BLACK POINT

HOTEL

BLACK POINT

JACQUELINE WEST

NEW YORK AMSTERDAM/ANTWERP LONDON
TORONTO SYDNEY/MELBOURNE NEW DELHI

An imprint of Simon & Schuster Children's Publishing Division
1230 Avenue of the Americas, New York, New York 10020

Jacket design by Karyn Lee

For information about special discounts for bulk purchases, please contact Simon & Schuster Special Sales at 1-866-506-1949 or business@simonandschuster.com.
Simon & Schuster strongly believes in freedom of expression and stands against censorship in all its forms. For more information, visit BooksBelong.com.
The Simon & Schuster Speakers Bureau can bring authors to your live event. For more information or to book an event, contact the Simon & Schuster Speakers Bureau at 1-866-248-3049 or visit our website at www.simonspeakers.com.
Interior design by Karyn Lee
The text for this book was set in Edita.
The illustrations for this book were rendered digitally.
Manufactured in the United States of America
First Edition
2 4 6 8 10 9 7 5 3 1
CIP data for this book is available from the Library of Congress.
ISBN 9781665981859
ISBN 9781665981873 (ebook)

For Ryan

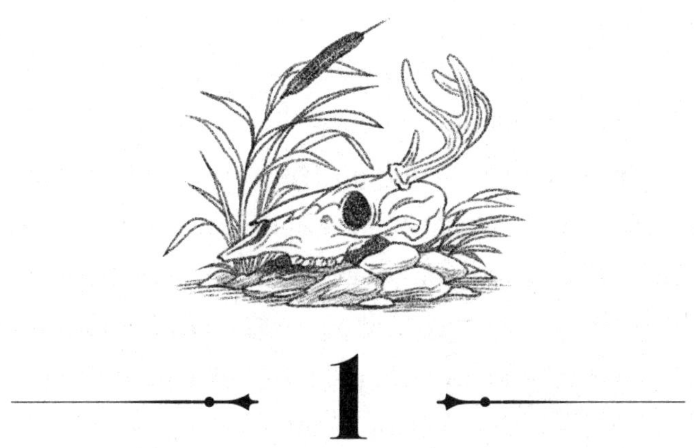

1

BLACK POINT IS GOING TO DROWN SOMEDAY.

They explained this to us back in ninth-grade science class: Eventually the river will rise and widen, or the big earthquake that experts keep predicting will finally snap through the riverbed like the dotted line on a graham cracker, and the whole town of Black Point will slide down into the water at last.

Sometimes I picture it there, at the bottom of the Mississippi. I can see the old hotel, Lou's Café, Grandpa's museum, all the redbrick churches and redbrick bars and stilt-braced wooden houses laid out on the riverbed just as they were on land, every wall and window flickering in greenish water-light. Black Point has balanced on the bluffs for a hundred and seventy years. It's withstood floods, blizzards, fires, the occasional avalanches that send boulders bouncing through the houses. Each trial has just made the town hold on tighter.

Even sinking into the Mississippi River couldn't destroy Black Point. I'm not sure anything could.

Grandpa's museum stands on Third Street, three blocks up from the river. Its official name is The Viking History Museum of Black Point, Wisconsin, but everyone here just calls it Frank's Place. Grandpa owns parts of several other local businesses—businesses that actually *make* money—and has used his income over the years to buy so many weird old things that they won't fit into our house anymore. Thus, the museum.

I would never use the word *thus* in conversation, by the way. Everyone around here thinks I read too much as it is. They also think I'm the teen girl version of my grandpa: history nerd, bookworm, devoted to this place.

There, at least, they're probably right.

Visitors don't expect a town the size of Black Point—population 893—to have a world-class collection of Viking paraphernalia. A lot of our objects are reproductions, of course, or they'd be under glass in the Smithsonian or something. But there are handmade weapons, drinking horns, model ships, carved runes, and scads of treasures brought here by our Swedish immigrant ancestors. It's over two million dollars' worth of stuff—I've seen the insurance paperwork. But really, the collection is priceless. Nothing creates history but time. And no one can buy that.

Tourists wandering in from the River Road always seem a little stunned by the place. The ones who expected a Viking *foot-*

ball museum are the most confused of all. They shuffle around for a while, staring at the ancient iron swords and the carvings to Odin and Freya and Thor, and then they wander back out again, drifting downriver along with the rushing green water.

I spend my weekends, my afternoons, and my summers at the museum. If it weren't for high school, I'd basically never leave. It's my favorite place in the world, I suppose because being there is like getting to live inside a thousand years all at once. I answer emails and make social media posts, climb ladders, sweep floors, and do whatever else Grandpa and the other Oldies can't. Or shouldn't. Since the last heart attack, Grandpa is supposed to take things easy, but he constantly forgets.

I never do.

Today, from my spot behind the front counter, I watch Grandpa saunter around the museum's main floor, smiling and nodding at the small knots of visitors. I monitor his pace. I watch his posture, still straight and sturdy. I check the smile that creases his always-stubbly cheeks.

Two older couples in khaki shorts have gathered around the big sword display. One of the men is talking loudly.

". . . Just imagine one of those naked berserkers running at you with this," I hear him saying to the other three, pointing at the replica sword in the center. "It says the original was found in a bog in Jutland. Probably part of a human sacrifice."

Grandpa saunters up to the group. "Human sacrifices happened every now and then," he says. "It seems to have been rare, but because wetlands were sacred to Norse people, evidence of sacrifices is frequently found preserved there. Often it was the weapons themselves that were sacrificed. Swords were so valuable, and so honored, they were given names. They were basically thought to have lives of their own."

"Hmm." The loud man gestures up at the sword—the one-of-a-kind, hand-forged, folded-steel sword. "Sure," he says. "That one looks like a 'Bob' to me."

The other khaki shorts laugh.

Grandpa grins. He's heard this one before. "Just let us know if you've got any questions," he says, turning and heading toward the front desk.

I watch him approach over the scuffed glass counter. I'm leaning on my elbows next to the register. Behind me, wearing their Viking Museum staff pins and seated on their usual folding chairs, are Les Gustafsson and Duane Bjorklund, who have known Grandpa since they all went to kindergarten together at Black Point's old one-room schoolhouse. Les is small and wiry and permanently dressed in plaid, and Duane is huge and bald and doughy everywhere but his hands, which are always carving a chunk of wood.

"Hey, you hear about Jerry Hallquist?" Les says as Grandpa reaches us.

I glance up.

Of course Grandpa has heard about Jerry Hallquist. We've all heard about Jerry Hallquist.

Jerry lived in Black Point his whole long life, running the family farm that's been here for ages. Last week a tornado ripped through the upper edge of town, yanking trees up by their roots, pouring rain on the already swollen river. It destroyed acres of crops, killed a couple of cattle, and pulled Jerry Hallquist's entire house into the air. People have been finding his possessions–old photos, papers, bits of faded clothes–for miles around. They found Jerry himself, or what was left of him, in the middle of a cornfield two days later. The farmer who spotted him thought he was a broken scarecrow.

"What about Jerry?" asks Grandpa. He circles around the counter to the rest of us, but he's still looking over his shoulder, across the museum floor.

Les folds his arms. "Mark's having him buried down in La Crosse."

"What?" says Grandpa.

Duane stops carving.

Mark Hallquist, Jerry's only son, owns a car dealership down in La Crosse now.

Deserter.

"Guess he thought it would be more convenient," says Les. "Or maybe he wanted him closer."

"Pretty sure Jerry would have wanted to be buried here," says Grandpa.

Duane nods. "He always said he'd leave this place in handcuffs or a coffin."

The Oldies chuckle softly.

"He's getting his way," says Grandpa.

"Hey, Lucia," says Les abruptly, angling toward me, "you still seeing that Jake Meier?"

I'm not thrown by the change of subject. The Oldies have five regular topics of conversation. They slide back and forth between them, adding tiny variations to things they've said ten thousand times, like a band playing a set of favorite songs. Subjects include:

1. The weather.
2. The weather in the past.
3. Things people in Black Point have done, said, or died of.
4. Who's selling what, who bought what, and who owned it in the past.
5. My love life.

I snort, turning on my elbow. "I was never 'seeing' Jake Meier."

"Hmm." Les shrugs. "Good-looking kid. Captain of the wrestling team. Seems pretty decent."

Les is a volunteer wrestling coach at the high school, which means he knows more about the locker-room habits of my male classmates than I'd ever want to.

"Didn't he take you to prom?" Duane puts in.

"We went to prom in a *group*," I tell them for what must be the fiftieth time. My insides are starting to squirm. "It was me and Cara and Bailey, Jake and Colton Norquist and Kyle Larson—"

"How about Kyle Larson?" says Les. "He's another decent-looking kid."

"Kyle Larson," I repeat. "Kyle Larson used to pull the legs off of grasshoppers one at a time and then throw their bodies at other kids, yelling, '*Hopper bomb!*'"

Les grins. "Aw, I bet that was at least a few months ago."

"Does it matter? Do you just outgrow being a sadistic idiot?"

"Well, Duane here has," says Les. "Almost."

Duane guffaws.

"Is Mark going to sell off the Hallquist place?" Grandpa asks, pulling the band back to the previous song. Thank goodness.

I tune out while the Oldies talk acres and prices and watch Grandpa instead. His skin looks normal today, tanned and dry, not grayish. His stance is missing the rigidity it gets when there's pain and he's trying to hide it. But he doesn't look relaxed either. His eyes keep flicking across the museum floor toward something in the distance.

Any little change in Grandpa is enough to fill my stomach with ice water.

I step closer to him. "Something wrong?"

Grandpa makes a gesture that's not quite a headshake, not quite a shrug. "Just not sure about one of our visitors."

The ice water warms a little. At least it isn't pain. I look back at the khaki group, who are now talking loudly beside a row of axes. "Which one?"

"Someone downstairs." Grandpa nods toward the top of the staircase. "You might not have noticed when he came in. He's been down there quite a while now."

Grandpa's eyes have always been sharper than mine. He's always first to spot the migrating cranes flying in over the river bottoms, or to notice the deer standing in the deep grass of a ditch, as still as if they'd already been shot and stuffed.

"What's wrong with him?" I ask.

"Just seems out of place." Grandpa answers. "A kid about your age, maybe eighteen, nineteen. In here by himself. Seems off."

A kid my age in here—a kid we don't already know—would be more than "out of place." It would be wrong.

"I'll go down and check," I say. Grandpa looks like he's going to argue, but I dodge out from behind the counter and cross the floor before he can stop me. "If anything's going on, I'll come straight back up."

Grandpa gives a nod.

I head down the steps.

The museum used to be a grocery store, decades ago. Grandpa fixed up the interiors so the wooden floors gleam, the walls are eggshell white, and the recessed lights glow bright enough to showcase every object. But even with the lights on, the lower floor is dimmer than the one above. If Black Point weren't built on such steep slopes, with basements that are half underground and half exposed to the river valley, it would be darker still.

I reach the foot of the staircase, moving softly. We've never had a crime at the museum, unless you count the misspelled swear words some kid scrawled in a bathroom stall, but if something is going on, I need to see it without being seen. I pad out onto the lower floor.

The basement holds most of our larger displays: racks of tunics and helmets for little kids to try on, three miniature ships, an open-walled longhouse. The space is quiet. No voices, no sounds but my own steps on the hardwood. The visitor must be in the corner with the replica village, tucked away behind the slant of the staircase.

I slip past the stuffed four-horned sheep in his glass box (I named him Olaf when I was five years old, so that's what his tag says: *Olaf, four-horned sheep*) and around the carved wooden chariot.

And there he is.

A black-haired boy in a gray T-shirt.

His back is to me. He's alone, staring down at the display about Black Point's founders. I've told Grandpa we should probably add "white" or "European" founders, because Dakota people have had settlements here for centuries. Grandpa always says that I can change it after he's gone. And I tell him that he'll never be gone.

I know exactly what's in that display case, below the map of Sweden with our founders' home village marked by a little flag. *Pocketknife, owned by Jan Lundberg, c. 1850. Compass, owned by Lars Angstrom, c. 1850. Firesteel, owned by Hans Hansson, c. 1800.*

Long Knife, owned by Varg Sorenson, date unknown.

The boy in the gray T-shirt isn't doing anything wrong. He's not doing anything at all. And still a bolt of cold electricity spears through me, like I've gone downstairs for a drink in the middle of the night and found a stranger standing in our living room.

Grandpa is right. This boy doesn't belong here.

I've never seen him before. He definitely doesn't go to school in Black Point. There are only ninety-four kids in the whole high school, and I could describe the hair and clothes and deodorant use of every single one. This boy's hair is longish and jagged, like it hasn't been cut in a while, but its last trim obviously wasn't at Dianne's Shear Beauty down on Second Street. His shirt doesn't have a team name or symbol on it. And he's wearing bracelets. Three of them, leather bands with small silver beads.

But the boy isn't our usual kind of tourist either. He's a few decades too young or a decade too old, and he's not part of a group that will pile back into a minivan and head off for burgers and ice cream afterward.

He's different.

He's wrong.

He steps to the right, turning slightly, and I duck behind a shelf.

Around its edge, I watch the boy examine some old farming tools. He doesn't touch anything. Doesn't hurt anything. He just looks, for a long, quiet moment, and then he turns toward the staircase, and I get my first glimpse of his face.

It doesn't look quite how I'd imagined it, which is how I realize I was imagining it in the first place. The features are a little less delicate. The eyebrows are heavier. The eyelashes are longer. It's an interesting face. An out-of-place face.

Without a glance in my direction, the boy heads up the staircase.

I wait until he's neared the top of the flight before dodging out from behind the shelf and tagging after him.

Upstairs, Grandpa and Duane are busy talking with a couple at the front desk—they're wearing Minnesota Vikings shirts, so they're in for some disappointment—and Les is out of sight. Grandpa's eyes flick toward the front door when the boy steps through it, then slice to me before going back to the tourists and their brochure.

I slip out the door behind the boy in the gray T-shirt.

I expect him to get into one of the cars parked along the slope of Third Street.

But he doesn't. The boy just turns to the left, striding away down the steep sidewalk like he already knows his way around. Like he knows exactly where he's going.

And suddenly I need to know too.

So I follow him.

I must have walked down Third Street five thousand times. Now I try to see it through a stranger's eyes. The steep, quiet street, still littered with leaf piles from last week's storm. Red-brick buildings pressed up against narrow sidewalks. Empty plate glass windows streaked with our reflections. I know what used to be behind each of these windows, which one was the hardware store, the antique shop, the bakery-café. All the things I'll help bring back to this town someday.

The boy doesn't pause anywhere. Not even at the intersections. He just strides across the streets like he's already sure there won't be any traffic. As I cross Eagle Avenue behind him, the storm-swollen river flashes into view, and the muddy breeze rises toward us, almost as thick and brown as the water itself.

We head down another block, across Falcon Avenue, into the oldest part of town—the part with three-story brick buildings with arched doorways and wooden balconies that sag out over the sidewalks. The boy walks toward the building on the next corner. The largest building in Black Point. The one with four stories of blank windows, and a broad stone stoop, and a huge set of double doors.

The old hotel.

It's been closed for more years than I've been alive, but everybody still calls it the hotel. Everybody knows the stories about the place: the bootleggers and old-time celebrities and politicians who stopped there on trips down the river, the bar where everyone in town used to gather. All the ghosts that haunt it.

I've never been inside. No one my age has. But its stories are ours, which makes the place ours, too.

When I stop on the far side of the street, leaving space between me and the boy in the gray T-shirt, he heads straight up the steps to the hotel's front doors. He takes a key from his pocket. Unlocks the door. Steps inside.

The double doors thump shut again.

I rock backward on my feet.

No one goes inside the hotel. Definitely not out-of-towners. Strangers. I feel a disoriented kind of anger, like I'm watching someone in a dream eat the food from my own plate.

This boy isn't from Black Point. He doesn't belong here, in the old, quiet, locked-up heart of it. Not unless he's a ghost himself.

I watch the hotel for a minute.

Finally, when I'm sure no one else is walking by, I run across the street after him.

March 29, 1986

Hey Matt,

Once I can buy some stamps, I'm going to mail this to Alicia's so dad won't see it. At least he won't if you're smart and leave it there instead of bringing it home. I'm guessing Alicia will read it too (HI, ALICIA!), so I won't write anything too embarrassing. About myself. You're fair game though. Ha ha.

I'm writing this in a letter because I sure as hell can't call the house, but I wanted you to know I'm okay. Plus it seems like a good idea for someone to know where I am. Even though I'm not totally sure myself.

So here goes.

When I took off from Madison, I headed northwest, sticking to country roads until I was lost in miles of cornfields, and it would have been pretty damn boring if I didn't have your tapes to keep me company. I stole your tapes, by the way. Metallica, Judas Priest, and Motley Crue. I'm really sorry. At least, I'm really sorry about taking Motley Crue, because that band sucks.

I'll send them all back when I can. Right now, I'm almost out of money, and the first thing I'll have to do when I get some is fix the truck. And now I'm telling everything out of order. I was never great at this writing stuff. Just ask Mrs. Fincher why she gave me that C minus.

Anyway, I slept the first night in the cab of the truck on a field road in the middle of nowhere. The next day, I finally found my way through the cornfields to the river road. So I was heading north, and I was somewhere halfway up the state when the truck started shuddering. I figured I must have broken a belt or something, because the steering was shot, and I just barely made it to the edge of the next little town.

I parked on a dead-end road leading into the woods just off another cornfield. Hopefully, nobody will notice if I leave the truck there for a couple days while I get things figured out. I can sleep in it again if I have to. And I'll probably have to. Just hope I don't hear banjos in the night. Ha ha.

Whatever happens, I'm not coming back.

I'll explain why someday. I wasn't going to stick around forever anyhow, working some crummy job and drinking my paycheck until I end up just like dad. I had to get the hell out when I got the chance. And being away from that town and that house and everything, even just for two days, has been freaking great.

No offense to you, Matt. You've got reasons to stay. (HI, ALICIA!) And you've always made better choices than me.

So, zero regrets. Except for taking your Motley Crue. I meant to take Iron Maiden.

I would've said goodbye in person, but once I had his truck keys and forty bucks in my pocket at the same time, I had to go.

I'll write more when I can.

Okay. You two can get back to making out now.

—Neil

2

BEHIND THE OLD HOTEL, BETWEEN ITS REDBRICK BACK WALL and the building that used to be Miller's Bar, there's a narrow strip of grass. By "grass," I mean crabgrass, weeds, and hollyhocks so huge and bristly, they look like they should sting. At the end of that strip of grass, there's a bolted door into what used to be the hotel kitchen. A small window is set high in the door. The rest of the hotel windows have been covered for years with ancient brown paper, but that little window never got covered at all.

So when the boy disappears through the front doors, I know exactly where to go.

I dodge through the crabgrass, past a patch of nettles, around the broken wooden cable spool that's been there forever, and step onto the crumbly back stoop. When we were younger, my best friends, Cara and Bailey, and I had to boost one another up to reach the window. Whoever was peering through it would narrate what they saw: the coal-dark hotel kitchen, the strange, lumpy shapes in the corners, the shadows that might be—no, that definitely *were*—moving. And then we'd all run off, screaming.

Now all I need to do to reach the little window is stand on my toes.

So that's what I'm doing, with my hands and chest braced against the old wooden door, when it suddenly swings outward.

I don't have time to register the light glowing inside, or the blur of motion behind the window, or the fact that everything inside looks different—and not just because I'm seeing it without being perched on another girl's knee. I stumble backward off the stoop, catching myself just before I fall into the scratchy hollyhocks.

The boy in the gray T-shirt stands in the doorway.

He doesn't look surprised to find me there.

He just gazes at me for a second. Then, without a change in expression, he says, "Regular or cherry?"

He might as well be speaking some other language.

"What?" I ask.

He holds up two cans, one in each hand. Regular and cherry Coke. "Which one?"

My head sloshes with questions—questions I might ask him, if I wanted to speak to him at all. But he asked me one first. And it's a question with only two answers.

I hear myself say, "Cherry."

He hands me the can.

It's cold.

I don't know how a can that came out of an abandoned hotel can be ice cold. For a second I just stand there, staring at the cherry Coke like someone who's never seen an aluminum can before.

He leans against the doorframe and opens his own drink. "You work at that museum?"

Annoyance sputters through my thoughts. Why should he get to ask *me* any more questions? How can he already know this about me when I don't know anything about him? And why is he staring at my chest, like a total—

I glance down. My Viking Museum badge is pinned to my shirt.

"Oh," I say. "Yeah." I clear my throat. "It's my grandpa's museum. I help run it."

The boy goes on gazing down at me, his face like a page printed in an unreadable language. "And you think I stole something?"

I frown up into his eyes. Their black-brown is fragmented with bits of yellow. Probably just reflections of the patchy sunlight. I have no idea what the look in them means: defensiveness, or amusement, or something else.

"No," I tell him. "It's just—teenage guys don't wander around the museum by themselves on summer weekends. And *nobody* goes in here." I point toward the hotel. "Not unless they're trespassing."

The boy takes a drink, but his gaze doesn't waver. "I live here."

"No, you don't." I sound like a five-year-old having an argument. But there's nothing else to say. This boy doesn't live here. I'd bet everything I know and everything I own on it.

"My aunt bought this place." He gestures into the darkness behind him. "I'm here for the summer, helping out, while she gets started with renovations."

There are so many impossible things in this speech that I can barely decipher it. The one word my brain grabs onto before turning it around and firing it back at him is–

"Renovations?"

"Yeah." The boy takes another drink. "She's turning it into a cidery. There will be local food and wine and other stuff too, but hard cider is her main thing."

Again, the words flood past me, swift and slippery as river muck.

There is no way his aunt, whoever she is, bought the biggest, best-known old building in town without anyone–or everyone–hearing about it.

The hotel belongs to Maeve Hansson. Everybody knows that. Maeve spent her entire life in the place, along with her mother, Jeanne, who had owned it since the days when cart horses were still tied to the stone posts outside. When Jeanne finally died decades ago, Maeve closed the business down and moved out. But she never even tried to sell it. There's no way Maeve would just hand it over. Not to someone who will rip it all apart. Not to someone who's not even from here.

The boy is still staring down at me from the doorway.

"So you *don't* really live here," I say, reaching after a few of his words. "You're just here for the summer. Then you'll go back to . . . wherever."

"Minneapolis."

"Minneapolis," I repeat, like it explains everything. Because it does.

My eyes drift past him into the dim interior, into a room I've only glimpsed through a dirty window in a locked door.

"This place has been closed for decades," I say aloud. "I've never even seen the inside."

"Do you want to?"

The boy turns to the side. Giving me room.

And even though I don't trust him, even though I don't believe that this is a gift he can offer me, I step straight up and through the open door.

I have no choice but to brush past him as I go. He's still holding the door open for me, bracing it with one arm. That's how I notice that he's just about my height—I'm tall, Mom is tall, Grandpa is tall—but his shoulders are broad, his torso a solid V. I keep my arms tight to my sides so they won't brush against his shirt.

Then we both step forward, the boy lets go of the door, and it thumps shut, sealing out the sunlight and sounds of Black Point.

Maybe because I've imagined the interior for so long, standing inside it at last feels inevitable. I look around the old kitchen—a long, narrow room, tinged gold by the sun that presses through the papered windows—and I see that the boy is telling the truth about one thing at least. Someone is renovating this place. Changing things.

Giant cardboard boxes are heaped in one corner. Two old stoves jut crookedly across the floor, bumped out of place by the gleaming industrial range. A huge brushed-steel refrigerator hums against the wall.

Now I know where the cold Coke came from.

"This is the kitchen, obviously." The boy moves past me, toward a swinging wooden door. "The bar is right through here."

I follow him.

Stepping through the door is like stepping into a yellowed photograph. I glance around in the dimness. High ceilings. Hanging red-gold lamps. A massive mirror-backed wooden bar lined by stools upholstered with dust. Small round tables and bentwood chairs. Ashtrays and water rings on the tabletops. I try to take in everything at once, like someone else might take it all away first.

"Nobody's touched this room in decades," says the boy as I move past him. "My aunt said when she first saw it, there were still cigarette butts in the ashtrays."

I step toward the bar. A stack of coasters printed with Black Point Hotel sits next to a heavy rotary phone. I lift the dust-furred receiver to my ear, half expecting to hear the whisper of voices. But of course there's nothing. Not even a dial tone.

"What would you do if someone spoke to you through that phone right now?"

I stiffen, jerking around. The boy is standing right beside me. His mouth is curled up on one side, but I don't know him well enough to tell if it's a smile or a smirk.

"I don't know," I tell him, setting the receiver back in its cradle. My hand leaves a print in its coat of dust. "Probably run out of here screaming and spilling cherry Coke everywhere."

His mouth splits into an actual smile. "Totally sensible reaction." He nods at my hand. "You still haven't opened your Coke, though."

"Oh." I've been hesitating all this time, not wanting to take anything else that he could offer me. But I know more about this place than he does. I have things he doesn't have.

"This place is haunted, you know." I finally open the can. "There are a hundred stories."

"Yeah?" The boy leans an elbow on the bar, still smiling. "I guess we haven't heard the local lore yet."

He waits, like he's sure I'm going to go on.

I look at his face. His eyebrows are angular and thick. His jaw is strong, with a tiny bit of stubble at the edges. Something about his eyes makes them look relaxed, almost sleepy, even when he's half smiling. I don't want to like this face. I keep myself from smiling back.

But I can let him in on a few stories. Maybe they'll even scare him off.

"The most famous ghost is the woman in white," I begin in my museum guide voice. "She was a bride who died here more than a hundred years ago, on what was supposed to be her wedding day. Afterward, people staying in the hotel would see the edge of a white skirt trailing out of sight around a corner, but when they ran after it, there'd be no one there. And then there was the bootlegger. He was hiding out here in the twenties, until one day, he just vanished. Rumor has it Al Capone had him killed. People sitting in this lobby used to hear jazz music playing from somewhere nearby, but no one could ever find where it was coming from. And there's the drowned man. He would leave wet footprints everywhere, in rooms no one was even using. There are more. A lot more."

The boy nods. His face is hard to read again. "I haven't seen anything ghostly myself," he says. "But if I do, I can let you know."

I can't tell if he's serious. If he's mocking me. If he's really promising to seek me out and talk to me again.

Not that I'd be hard to find.

"So, your aunt's *renovating* this whole place?" I just barely let the line sound like a question.

"Yeah." He pushes away from the bar, stepping forward. "This space will be the big cider-tasting room and bistro. Eventually she's going to do the upper floors too, so it can be a little inn."

He nods toward the wide wooden staircase at the far end of the room. "It's just us living up there for now."

"You're living *in* the hotel?" The impossibility of this—where I am, who I'm with, what he's saying—crashes over me again. "How could you be living here without everybody in town knowing?"

He shrugs. "We haven't moved everything in yet. And we haven't met too many people."

My eyes wander away from him, back to the wooden staircase. Part of me wants to believe that I just saw a filmy white skirt trailing up the top steps, but the rest of me knows that I'm just wishing.

I take a drink. "What's it like up there?"

His half smile curves back. "Mildewed."

"Do you and your aunt each have, like, six rooms to yourself?"

"We could. We each just took one for now."

"And you've already been cleaning it up? Moving things around?"

"A little bit." He steps toward the staircase. "Do you want to see?"

Do I want to see? Yes, I do. Because I know, as I take another look around this big, dim, gold-faded room, that this will be my only look at the old hotel. That everything here will change. It's already changing, already becoming something that erases everything it used to be.

But going up to a bedroom in an empty old hotel with some

boy I don't even know would be moronic. Wouldn't it? Probably. Yes.

"No," I say out loud. "I should get back."

"Sure." The boy changes course easily, moving toward the front doors. "Well—it was nice to meet you. Not that I really did."

He turns back and puts out a hand.

I switch my can from right to left before taking it. His grip is warm and dry. Mine is cold and clammy. We shake.

"Max Nazarian," he says.

I don't know any other Maxes. I definitely don't know any other Nazarians.

"I'm Lucia. Sorenson." I tag on the last name as an afterthought. Anyone who knows my first name usually knows my last name too. Along with who my family is. Where I live. Everything.

"Lu-see-ah," he repeats. "Italian?"

"Swedish. Like everything else around here."

"Lucia," he says again. "I'll see you around, then."

I shrug. "Probably. It's not a big place."

"I've noticed." He smiles again—the full, warm smile this time. "Still, it will be good to know somebody who can give inside advice."

"Inside advice?" I repeat, following him closer to the doors. "Don't get pizza from the Badger Hole."

He looks confused.

"It's a bar," I tell him. "Two blocks up."

"Oh. Not an actual hole full of pizza-making badgers."

And now I can't stop myself fast enough. I smile back at him. "No. Not that."

I step quickly toward the doors so he can't get a good look at my face.

He pushes the front door open for me. I step out of the gold-tinted, dust-scented hotel back into the Black Point of today, with its steep streets and river sounds and smells of pavement and mud.

"Thanks for the tip," says Max.

"Sure." I pause on the steps, not looking at him, but nodding up at the four stories of the old brick hotel above us instead. "Good luck."

Then I turn and stride away. The high water of the river tumbles after me.

March 31, 1986

Hey Matt,

Well, the truck and I are still stuck here.

I spent the last two nights sleeping in the cab. It's been freaking FREEZING for March, but at least nobody chased me off with a deer rifle. And I've spent the days wandering around this whole town, which doesn't take long, looking for Help Wanted signs.

No luck.

By yesterday afternoon, I was starting to wonder whether I should try to pawn your tapes, or whether I should give panhandling a try. I ended up going to the laundromat instead, because I figured if I ever DID find an opening, nobody would hire someone who stank as bad as I did after three days without a shower anyway. While I was washing all the clothes I could take off without getting arrested, I ended up helping the lady who runs the place move a couple of machines around. She asked me where I was from and what I was doing here and so on. I told her I was from Milwaukee, that I was passing through, and that I was looking for work so I could fix my truck. Which was only about eighty miles from being true.

She looked at me in my ratty boxer shorts and

asked, "What kind of work?" like I might be some low-rent hustler or something. (BET YOU'RE ENJOYING THAT IMAGE, ALICIA.) I said I could do construction, dishwashing, yard work, whatever needed doing. Then she asked if I had family around, or if I knew anyone in town, or if I had a place to stay. I told her no to everything, and maybe that made her feel sorry for me, because all the sudden she went, "I think we can help you out with everything at once," and hauled me down the block in a T-shirt and jeans from the lost-and-found box.

So that's how I ended up at the Black Point Hotel.

Don't picture the Hilton or anything. It's more like an old bar with an apartment house on top of it. There's good food though. And my room and board are covered.

I'll write more later. Right now I'm about to pass out, and I'm looking forward to a night of sleep without my nose hairs freezing.

Hope you're doing all right. Hope dad isn't taking any of this out on you.

Don't tell him where I am, all right? Don't tell anybody.

—Neil

3

Lou's Café stands on Second Street. It's wedged between Bergquist Jewelers, which is only open three days a week, and an empty office with a yellowed For Rent sign in the front window and crooked metal blinds across the door. Between these two quiet spots Lou's is bright and busy, with red awnings and glowing neon signs and window boxes full of marigolds. It looks like the one working bulb in a string of tired Christmas lights.

Lou is wiping down the pie case when I step through the front door, but she gives me a quick smile as I pass. Lou's is the kind of place where you seat yourself. The staff already knows where you're going to sit and what you're going to order anyway.

The Oldies are in their usual five fifteen spot: a long table tucked behind the bend in the counter. A cluster of framed photos hangs above them, group shots of all the regulars who have held court here over the decades. The one just above Grandpa's usual chair shows Les, Duane, Chuck Lundberg, and Grandpa–the surviving regulars–smiling up at the camera, along with Jeanne Hansson, who owned the hotel, Chuck's late wife Marina, and Al Bjorklund, Duane's dad. Lou has drawn little ballpoint halos over the heads of the dead.

Duane never married. Chuck and Marina never had kids. Les's wife divorced him decades ago and took their two children down to Winona with her. Grandpa is the only Oldie with descendants still living in Black Point.

I'm the only new branch on the tree. I need to be sturdy.

Les is speaking as I approach the table. I hear him saying something like "When the water reaches the mouth . . ." but then his eyes catch me, and he breaks off. "There she is!" he says in a louder, brighter tone.

Chuck gives me a wink. "Hey there, Frankie."

Chuck has called me Frankie ever since I was tiny. Sometimes the other Oldies do it too. They say I'm so much like my grandpa, they should have just named me after him. And that "Frankie" is easier to pronounce than "Lucia," anyway.

Grandpa grins, pulling out the chair next to his, pouring coffee from the thermal carafe into the cup that's already waiting for me.

"So, did you run that kid out of town?" asks Les.

Everyone guffaws.

"Just halfway across it." I sit and grab a creamer from the dish.

"Yeah?" says Duane. "Straight into the river, then?"

I laugh along with them this time. Les's laugh is a sharp wheeze. Duane's is soft, Chuck's is gruff. Grandpa's is loud and clear and one of my favorite sounds anywhere.

"No." I tug the foil from the drum of creamer. "Just into the hotel."

The words are out before I realize how suggestive they sound. My cheeks start to prickle.

I rush on before anyone can hassle me. "He says his aunt bought it."

Everyone goes silent. No more teasing now. The faces of the Oldies are suddenly serious, disbelieving, their eyes intent on me.

"His aunt bought it?" Chuck's thick eyebrows pull into a scruffy ledge. Chuck is tall and big-boned, but everything else about him—except his eyebrows—has started to shrink. Now he looks like a knobby coatrack draped in flannel. "You mean Maeve sold it?"

"I guess so." I pour the cream into my cup, watching it sink through the dark coffee like inhaled smoke.

"No way Maeve would sell," says Les.

Duane sips his coffee. The yellow ceiling lights slick his bald head. "Who knows what Maeve will do?"

"She can't *need* to sell it," says Chuck. "She owns it outright. Plus her house and her store."

"Who did you say she sold it to?" Grandpa asks me.

"That kid's aunt. He says she's going to turn it into a cidery."

The words land with a thud. Like I've plopped a dead fish in the middle of the table.

Les's forehead wrinkles.

Chuck snorts.

"Where are they from?" asks Grandpa. "Did they say?"

"Minneapolis."

There's another silent thud.

Maeve didn't just sell. She sold to people who won't even live here. Who don't belong in Black Point at all.

"What's their name?" Duane asks.

"I didn't meet the aunt," I say. "They might not have the same last name. I don't know."

"What's *his* name, then?" Grandpa prompts.

I sip my coffee. I've had so much coffee at Lou's over the years that I can barely taste it.

"Max," I answer at last. "Max Nazarian."

Grandpa and Les look at me. Duane and Chuck look at each other.

"Sounds Middle Eastern," says Les.

I shrug. "He just said they were from Minneapolis."

There's another brittle pause.

"If Maeve wanted to sell," Grandpa says, "she could have sold the place to me, like I've been asking her to do for thirty years. Not to out-of-towners."

"At least it means people are coming instead of just leaving." I say it quietly. But I shouldn't have said it at all.

Les clears his throat. "I'd better stop by Maeve's place tonight. Try to see what's going on."

Les is Maeve's second cousin—distant enough that you'd never match them up without knowing it already, close enough that he's got a slightly better chance of understanding her than the rest of us.

"Well, it's already done," I say, not sure why I feel like I'm defending something. "These people have moved in. They're living there."

Now the Oldies all trade looks. Chuck swirls the dregs of his coffee. Duane scratches two rough fingers across the arch of his shiny head.

"We got that tour group coming down tomorrow still?" Les asks Grandpa after a long beat.

"From the old folks' home." Grandpa nods. "Always a barrel of laughs."

The Oldies go on, pushing the conversation back toward its usual tracks. But the rhythm feels unsteady now. The notes are out of tune.

At last all the old guys stand up and throw a few dollar bills on the tabletop. Lou doesn't bother writing checks for us.

"See you tomorrow!" she calls as we head out the door.

Les and Chuck turn left, down the hill. Duane lifts his bulk into the cab of his truck. Grandpa and I head right, up the steep slope of Redtail Avenue.

Above us the bluffs are thick with green deepening to near

black in the patches of pines. The highest, narrowest jut of rock–the black point that got us our name–looms over us, gazing down at the river that has kept it company for ages. The rocks, the woods, the water. I've seen it all thousands of times, and it still makes my heart lift like opening wings.

Grandpa and Mom and I live in an old house at the end of Fourth Street, not far from the library and city hall. The house is yellowish brick, with an L-shaped porch, cobbled walkways, and an old, leaky fountain in the front yard. Every summer at least one tourist couple comes straight up to the front door thinking it's a bed and breakfast.

Mom is in the kitchen when Grandpa and I step inside. She's still dressed in her librarian clothes, which are a less-wrinkled version of the dresses she wears around the house.

"Supper should be hot in two minutes," she says, turning to give us a shared smile. "I hope you didn't fill up on pie at Lou's."

"Naw," says Grandpa. "They were out of all the good kinds."

The three of us sit around the kitchen table. The evening light is starting to slide from gold to rose, and the ivy that twines over the kitchen windows glows with falling sun. Down the hill, on Main and Second and Third Streets, everyone else in Black Point is sitting down for their own suppers, turning on their TVs, sinking into their saggy armchairs. And, below us all, the river rolls past, swift and thick, inching higher.

Mom and Grandpa are chatting about a next-door neighbor when my phone hums.

It's a text from Cara.

Do you know if you're coming down to Madison this weekend yet?

Can't, I type back. *Way too busy here.*

She's writing back before I'm even finished. *Bailey's coming for sure. And we're not just going to do the school tour, we'll explore, hang out on State Street. You need to come. It will be FUNNN.*

I clench my teeth.

One more year and Cara and Bailey will head off to college in Madison, or Eau Claire, or Milwaukee, leaving Black Point behind. They talk about it so much, sometimes it's like they've already left.

And I'm still here.

No, I write back. *Sorry.*

Four seconds pulse by.

Then Cara types, *K.*

I know her well enough to read the real message.

She's mad.

"No phones at the table, Luce," says Mom, scooping up a forkful of hotdish.

"Sorry." I drop my phone into my lap. "It's just Cara asking me about going to Madison tomorrow. I already told her I can't come."

"Oh, you should go along! That would be great for you!" Mom says lightly. But it's false lightness. Lots of weight underneath.

"I can't," I repeat. "Summer weekends are the museum's busiest times."

"I'm sure your grandpa can spare you for one weekend. Right, Dad?"

Next to me, Grandpa gives a quick nod. He stays scrupulously silent.

"I don't need to tag along on some campus tour," I say. My voice gets sharper, even though I'm trying to keep it smooth. "I have things to do here."

"Sure," Mom whisks onward. "Oh—Lisa Ekberg came in today, too. She said someone from Minneapolis is moving down and refurbing the old hotel. Turning it into a winery."

"A cidery," I say without thinking.

Grandpa fixes his eyes on his plate.

Mom turns toward me. "You know about this?"

"I just heard today," I answer. Grandpa's silent presence fills the corner of my eye. "The owner's nephew came into the museum. It's going to be a cidery and bistro, I guess."

"Well. That'll be a big change." Mom leans back in her chair. "What about the people?"

I swallow a bite. "What about them?"

"What are they like? What are their names?"

"Nazarian," says Grandpa shortly.

"Nazarian," Mom repeats. I can see her doing just what the Oldies did, paging through a list of familiar names in her head, looking for connections. Finding none. "Sounds Armenian. Or Persian, maybe."

Grandpa and I don't answer.

Grandpa and the Oldies didn't set foot in the Catch of the Day Café after the Rasmussons sold it to that couple from Rochester. And they never bought a beer in the short-lived Irish bar someone from the Cities tried to open in the Millers' old place, either. People who sweep in here and try to change things, things they were never and will never be part of, usually disappear again pretty fast. Driftwood on the river.

That will be the boy from the hotel soon enough. There's no point getting to know him. There's no point even remembering his name.

Max.

"A cidery," says Mom, filling the quiet. "That place must need some serious repairs. I'm sure with all the flooding we've had . . ."

Mom is still talking when Grandpa rises to his feet. He takes his plate to the sink, rinses it, and slots it into the dishwasher. He leaves the kitchen without speaking again.

My phone buzzes in my lap.

I expect it to be Cara, back with another argument. But the top of the screen reads, "Bailey Lundberg."

Bonfire in the woods tonight! Want to come?

I hesitate.

It would be stupid of me to throw away all my remaining chances to be with my friends before they vanish for real. Wouldn't it? Especially when I have no real excuse.

Sure, I write back.

Yay! Pick you up at 8!

Mom watches me slide the phone into my pocket.

"Sorry again," I tell her. Then I add, "I'm going out with Bailey tonight," before she can ask. Because she will. "We'll probably just hang out in the woods."

"It looks like more storms are on the way." Mom scrapes a last bit of hotdish across her plate. "Be safe out there."

"We will. I promise. If there's lightning, we'll shelter under the *very tallest* tree."

Mom purses her lips. "Smart aleck."

Together, we get up to rinse our own plates.

"Hey!" Bailey chirps as she steers her ancient Honda down the slope of Eagle Avenue. "Are you coming with us to Madison this weekend?"

I almost growl out loud.

"No," I tell her. "I already told Cara too. We're way too busy at the museum."

Bailey doesn't look at me. "Sure. The museum."

The words are light, but there's something in her tone that stings like a snapped rubber band.

"What?" I ask. "You know they need me there. Cara's already mad at me about it, which is totally unfair."

"Luce, I'm sure she's not *mad*, it's just—" Bailey pauses, turning onto the highway that leads out of town. Above us, a mass of clouds has turned the sky to black. "It seems like everything's been different with you lately."

"*I'm* not the one who's different," I shoot back. "I'm still right here. Exactly who I've always been."

"You think you're exactly the same? The same as when you were a kid? The same as when we met in toddler story time at the library?"

Bailey can make me smile even when I'm annoyed. "Okay," I admit. "I'm taller. Less drooly. Otherwise pretty much the same."

"Me too," says Bailey. "Better vocabulary, bigger clothes. But still me."

I run my fingers along the rubber strip at the base of the window. Beyond the glass, the black sky roils.

"Don't you think everything is going to change when you leave?" I ask softly.

Bailey makes a little surprised noise. "It's not like I'll never come back."

"Sure. Maybe." I press on the glass with my fingernails. "I just wonder sometimes . . . How much can you change without becoming a completely different person?"

She doesn't answer this.

The quiet that winds around us feels like a thinning thread. Something fraying. Preparing to break.

We bump off the highway onto the dirt road that leads into the Norquists' woods. All along the horizon, lightning pulses behind the clouds, tearing gold seams through the dark.

"Maybe we should just hang out at Lou's Café tonight," I say.

Bailey laughs, her usual brightness coming back. "That storm is miles off. Plus we're not seventy-five years old."

"Well, *I* am," I tell her as she pulls onto the shoulder. Ahead of us, between the tree trunks, flames leap and flicker. "Seventy-four, actually. But my birthday's coming up on Monday, remember?"

Bailey laughs again and climbs out into the guttering light.

We tromp through the trees into a small clearing. A few guys are gathered beside a fire: Jake Meier, Colton Norquist, Kyle Larson. They grin and wave and shout our names.

You can't help but smile back at anyone who's that happy to see you. I've never been as close to Jake or Colton or grasshopper-torturing Kyle as I am—or was—with Cara and Bailey. But the guys are from here. They'll stick around. Maybe that's enough.

"Hey, Lucia." Jake appears beside me. "Want one?" He pushes a can of energy drink into my hands before I can answer.

I glance around. "Where's everybody else?"

"It's just us tonight," Colton speaks up. He's gangly and fast-talking, and I've literally never seen him without Jake or Kyle right by his side. "We're being exclusive."

I snort-laugh. "How fancy."

"We only invited a few people," Colton goes on. "The ones whose families have lived here forever. Tonight we just wanted to be with the people who really know and love this place, you know?"

The words hit me like raindrops on cinders. Maybe we share more than I gave the guys credit for.

"What about Cara?" I ask.

"Her family's not *from* here, remember?" says Bailey. "They moved up from La Crosse when we were in first grade."

"Oh. Right." I raise my drink. "Then—cheers to really knowing this place."

Everyone else raises theirs. I spot Kyle pouring something from a small glass bottle into his can, then passing the bottle to Colton. Kyle is one of those people with a source for everything he shouldn't have.

Jake has edged a bit closer to me.

I glance at him in the firelight. He's about my height, ropy in that wrestling team way, sort of hard and condensed. His hair is blondish. His eyes are pale blue. Most of the time he's like the coffee at Lou's—I've seen him so many times, I can barely see him at all. But now that I'm looking more carefully, I spot a change on his face, the features solidifying, like a piece of wood being whittled away until everything extra is gone. It's what he's going to look like as a man.

I take a small step away.

There's a flash of lightning, closer now, bright enough to make the bonfire seem dim.

"There aren't supposed to be any tornadoes tonight," says Jake, guessing what we're probably all thinking.

"More rain's coming, though," says Colton. "I told you: This is going to be a bad summer. You all heard about Jerry Hallquist, right?"

"Everybody's heard about Jerry Hallquist," I say softly.

"I'm just saying," Colton plows on, "I bet he won't be the only one. I bet we'll have at least one more tornado touch down. And I'd bet ten thousand bucks the town's going to flood."

Kyle laughs, even though we're talking about a dead man and years of black mold. "Dude, you don't have ten thousand bucks."

"You should bet what you *do* have," Bailey teases. "A broken dirt bike and a huge collection of Pokémon cards."

Colton gives her a fake glare.

"He's right," Jake picks up. "Lots of rain up north. There'll be flooding for sure."

There's another flicker of lightning chased by a rush of wind. Branches above us lash and rustle. The fire gutters.

"When did you guys become meteorologists?" Bailey asks. "Have you all been extra bored this summer?"

Jake laughs, Kyle frowns, and Colton shakes his head.

"It's not about the weather," Colton says. "It's about the place."

"We've been talking," Jake puts in. "About what we should do if things keep getting worse."

If things keep getting worse. I picture Black Point sliding down the slope into the river, green-brown waves closing over its rooftops. Swallowing it all. My lungs go tight, like I'm already holding my breath.

"So, you've figured out a way to halt climate change?" I say, and it comes out more bitter than I mean it to.

But the guys don't seem to mind. Or notice.

"Kind of," says Colton. "I mean, not everywhere. But we know something that might help."

"Or at least won't hurt," says Jake.

"Aw, I think it might hurt." Kyle laughs. "But just for a second."

Colton and Jake laugh too.

There's another crash of wind, cool and damp with coming rain.

"Okay, before it starts pouring," says Bailey, folding her arms, "what are you guys talking about?"

Colton's eyes brighten. "We—"

"Hang on. Before we tell you, everybody has to promise never to tell anybody else. And everybody needs to take a drink," says Kyle, waving the glass bottle.

"I'm driving," says Bailey.

"And I don't really want your nasty schnapps," I tell him.

"It's vodka," Kyle shoots back. "And it's *symbolic*."

"You mean ceremonial," says Colton.

"Whatever." Kyle shoves the bottle into Jake's hands.

He drinks and passes to me. I don't want to touch what Jake's lips have just touched. It feels wrong: too close, like wet breath on the side of your neck.

But everyone is waiting.

I take one quick ceremonial sip. It tastes like nail polish remover.

"So," says Colton once the bottle has reached him, "we were talking about Viking rituals one day, after we watched that movie—what's it called—*The Norseman*?"

I heave a sigh loud enough that everyone can hear it, even over the fire. All eyes flick to me. "You know most of the ritual stuff in movies like that is crap, right?"

"Yeah," says Colton impatiently. "That's the point."

Jake grins at me. "We've all been to your grandpa's museum way too many times not to know *that*."

"But that's how we got talking about what *did* really happen," Colton goes on. "How they'd make offerings to the gods, or to nature, like, to *appease* them. To stay safe."

"My Grandpa Bruce was telling me how kids used to do that here," Kyle says, finally looking almost serious. "Whenever things got bad, with storms and floods and stuff. A few of them who'd lived here forever and passed down those traditions would get together in the woods and have a bonfire. Make an offering."

I can feel the doubt practically dripping down my face.

Sure, maybe this happened. People around here love to play Viking. But they can usually tell the difference between reenactment and reality. The wind hisses; scents of smoke and mud lash through the air.

"Anyway, the three of us talked about it," says Colton, "and we thought the least we can do is try, right? Better than the town getting wrecked." He glances toward Jake, like he's waiting for permission. Jake gives a little nod. Colton tips his head toward the trees. "So . . ."

I follow his eyes. Parked at the shadowy edge of the clearing is Kyle's pickup truck.

The guys stride toward it.

Bailey nudges my arm, wearing a bemused little smile. Together we follow them out of the ring of firelight.

Kyle opens the tailgate.

It takes a few seconds before I can tell what I'm seeing. It's sprawled in the middle of the truck bed: a lump of something soft and gray brown, with darker parts jutting out beneath it like broken sticks. The fire shivers, and light glints in its eyes.

Because it has eyes.

It has a head, and a limp neck, and a motionless body. And below that, trickling around the open tailgate, a pool of what is obviously blood.

"Oh my god," says Bailey from behind me. "Holy . . ."

"Holy sheep?" Kyle suggests.

Bailey bursts out a laugh. *"Holy SHEEP!"*

A cold wave rises up my body, prickling in each knob of my spine.

"Oh my god," I say too, but it comes out so small, even I can barely hear it. I clear my throat. "Where did you . . ."

I don't finish.

Kyle answers anyway. "Oleson's farm."

"They gave you a sheep?"

He shrugs, grinning. "They don't know it's gone."

I squint down at the creature. There's a bullet hole in the side of its head, so dark and wet that it looks bottomless. I press my fingertips to my own temples. "You mean, you took a gun—"

"A hunting rifle," Colton corrects me, speaking slowly. Like *I'm* the idiot.

"You took a *rifle* into someone else's field, and you shot one of their sheep."

"We paid for it," says Jake. As if this is the problem. "We left an envelope of cash in the shed."

"Oh my god," I say again. "You're lucky *you're* not the ones who got shot."

And then, because it's all so ridiculous, and so stupid, and because we're all still alive, I hear myself sputter out a laugh. Bailey joins in, and soon we're all laughing, doubled over, wiping our eyes, and the trees whip around us, and the wind drags strands of my own hair through my teeth.

When we can't laugh anymore, we all haul the sheep out of the truck, its body swinging awkwardly between us as we shout directions to one another. We heave it up onto the bonfire, which sends a swirl of embers into the wind. The sparks streak around us for a second, like a swarm of stinging insects, before winking out.

"Now what?" says Kyle, a little out of breath.

"We should say something. Right?" asks Colton. "Something *ceremonial.*"

"Right." Jake beckons all of us in. "We should join hands."

Everybody obeys. Jake is the kind of person people do that for. He has that quiet confidence, the ease that comes from thinking everything he wants is already his.

There aren't enough of us to encircle the fire, but we make a line with Colton at one end, Kyle at the other. Somehow Jake has ended up beside me again. His palm is hot and sticky against mine.

"Go ahead," he tells Colton.

"All right." Colton lifts his free hand, palm up, and raises his voice. "This is an offering to the forces of nature."

I have to stifle another laugh.

"We honor you tonight. We ask you to preserve our home. Protect this place, and the people who belong here, no matter what comes."

He yanks Bailey's hand upward, and she pulls mine, and I pull Jake's, and now we're all standing there, our joined hands in the air, while the smell of burning wool and flesh ripples in the red light around us.

Everyone keeps silent.

I try not to look straight into the fire. I don't want to see what's happening inside the flames. What's being revealed. What's falling apart. But when you're standing right beside a bonfire, it's hard to look away.

Finally we lower our hands and peel them apart. And we genuinely have to peel them, because our hands are coated with sticky, drying blood; blood that I didn't even notice in the dimness. I can still feel the heat of Jake's hand. The way it stuck to mine, like we'd been smeared with glue.

There's another wordless moment.

It's broken by the deep rumble of thunder.

"I should really be getting home," I murmur to Bailey.

She looks grateful for the excuse. "Me too. We should all get out of here before it starts pouring."

Colton nods. He looks a little dazed suddenly, like he's just waking up. "Yeah. We'll just stay to watch until this . . . burns down."

Bailey and I stumble toward the road.

"Remember, no telling anybody!" Kyle, the only one who's still grinning, shouts after us.

The drive home is quiet. Bailey keeps her eyes on the road, our headlights a tiny silver patch that we're chasing through the dark.

We've just pulled up to my house when the sky rips open.

"Good night!" I shout over the pouring rain as I clamber out. "Drive safe!"

"See you soon!" she shouts back, or I think she does. In a second her voice and the sound of the car are washed away by the hiss of the storm.

I race up the walkway to the door. Still, I'm soaked by the time I fling myself inside.

The first floor of the house is empty. It's late, after midnight; Mom and Grandpa must have gone to bed. They left the small kitchen light burning for me. I crank the hot-water faucet. Then I scrub and scrub and scrub my hands until the skin feels raw and slick as plastic. I'm still scrubbing when I hear a thud behind me.

I spin around so fast that I splash water across the countertop.

Grandpa steps into the kitchen.

We both give a backward jerk.

"Oh. Jeez," I gasp, putting one wet hand over my chest. "You startled me."

"Vice versa," says Grandpa, a little breathless.

I never want to be the reason that Grandpa's heart misses a beat. "I'm sorry. I didn't—"

Grandpa waves me away. He tugs off his soaked windbreaker and hangs it on the peg by the back door. There's something hurried and jerky about his movements. Something only I might notice. "Naw, naw, I'm fine," he says. "Just didn't expect anybody to still be up."

"I just got home," I say, stiffening with another spear of guilt. I put both hands behind me and lean back against the wet counter. "Where were you?"

"We got into a long talk down at Chuck's." He grins. "You know how long Chuck's talks can get."

There's a rumble and flash from beyond the kitchen windows. I picture rain pounding the surface of the river, sluicing down the hillsides. The water climbing higher.

"Well . . . I'm really tired." I slide my hands into my back pockets. "I should get to bed."

"Sure." Grandpa grins at me again. "Night, Luce."

I dart out of the kitchen. I catch the scent of smoke—must be Les's cigarettes—wafting from Grandpa's clothes as I slip past.

I'm sure I reek of smoke too. Tomorrow, early, I'll take a long shower.

Shut inside my bedroom, I strip off my soggy clothes and roll them into a ball. I'm going to do the same thing with the memories of this whole stupid night: roll them up, stuff them into the wash, and let time and water rinse everything clean.

I glance out the window as I climb into bed. Through the rain-smeared windowpane I can see the scattered lights of town tumbling down the slope toward the river. There are the blurry porch lights of Second Street, the red-and-white blaze of the gas station, the misty streetlights of Main. The silhouette of the hotel stands out, sharp and peaked, against the gray ripple of the river. For the first time I can remember, a light glimmers in one of the upper rooms.

I wonder if the light is his. If I'm looking at Max right now, even though I can't see him. Or if all I'm seeing is a ghost.

April 2, 1986

Hey Matt,

You know what I've been thinking? If I was smarter, maybe I'd have stuck it out in Madison for another two months until they handed me my actual diploma. I mean, being able to prove you graduated from high school seems like a good thing, right?

Or maybe not. It's not like I could show it to anyone, since I sure as hell can't use my real name. And it's not like you need a diploma to wash dishes. Maybe the fact that I can't make up my mind just proves how dumb I am. Another reason I need that diploma.

Ha ha.

Anyway, I've worked my first three full days at the Black Point Hotel, and I think I've already gained ten pounds. The ladies here can COOK. Jeanne and Maeve Hansson—that's the mother and daughter who run this place, and who look and sound like identical twins who were born thirty years apart—give me all my meals for free. Plus they do my laundry, they're going to pay me in cash, and they're even going to mail these letters for me. So I pretty much lucked out.

Apparently Maeve is psychic or something too.

Everybody says so. The first time I met her, she stared at me for so long, I thought there was something wrong with her. But then she said, "You're a Taurus, aren't you?" So maybe she is a little bit psychic. Then she put me right to work.

The Hanssons make huge batches of one or two main dishes for every meal, plus some sides and dessert. There's no menu or anything. It's more like cooking for a big family. The regulars are a bunch of locals who come in for supper every single night or who live right here in the hotel because there aren't any normal apartment buildings in a town this small. Everybody knows each other. And I'm the stranger who just wandered into their house.

I get a lot of stares and a lot of questions, at least from the friendlier people. They want to know where I'm from, what I'm doing here, if I've got family nearby. I can't exactly tell them that I'm not even eighteen until next month and that I ran away from home with my dad's truck. So as far as everyone here knows, my name's Neil Schmidt. I picked Schmidt because every town in Wisconsin has a Schmidt, right? I told them I'm from Milwaukee and I'm just working my way down the river, trying to get some experience and see a little of the country before I settle down somewhere.

Sounds pretty responsible, doesn't it? Smart, even. Like a guy who doesn't need his dumb diploma at all.

Speaking of smart and dumb, though. I've got to tell you something. You should read this by yourself, so if you're with Alicia right now (HI, ALICIA), stop and put it in your pocket and wait till you're alone. You can make up some lie or something for her later. (HI, ALICIA. YOU'RE NOT SUPPOSED TO BE READING THIS ANYMORE, SO DON'T GET OFFENDED OR ANYTHING.)

Okay. You know how I'd been working at Meyer's Warehouse for the last six months? My manager was the owner's nephew, this guy named Mick. He started having me help with extra jobs, off the clock. Just more sorting and loading and stuff. He'd pay bonuses in cash, get burgers or pizza delivered at the end of the night. He was always super nice to me. I didn't know what it all meant. I guess this proves I'm stupid, that I didn't ask questions.

It took me a while to realize he was skimming stuff. Taking boxes here and there, having me process them, sending them off to someplace else. He'd bring in some other guys after hours in big white vans, and they'd load everything up and take off again.

By the time I figured it out, I'd been helping Mick for months. And then one day I heard him talking with his uncle. They were talking about the missing stuff, and Mick was acting all puzzled. Then he told Mr. Meyer that he guessed a couple of his employees could be running a racket or something. And he mentioned my name.

He was going to throw me under the bus.

I can see you shaking your head, Matt.

I was already planning on getting out of Madison, like I said. But this put the gas in my tank. If I turned on Mick, he'd send those big guys in the vans after me. And if the whole thing got turned over to the cops, I'd probably be eighteen by the time it got to court or whatever, so they'd try me as an adult. And dad's sure as hell not going to hire some lawyer to help me out.

So. Yeah. I guess I'm on the lam, except that sounds way more exciting than washing dishes in a hotel. Can you become a criminal just by being dumb? I don't know. Maybe you can figure out the answer.

You'd better burn this letter now.

Just wanted you to know why it matters that no

one knows where I am, and why I can't come back. On top of the whole stealing dad's truck thing.

Take care, Matt. Don't do anything I would do. Ha ha.

—Neil

4

MOST PEOPLE HAVE NEVER HELD A BATTLE AXE.

They've seen them on-screen, in the fists of charging Vikings, and they think they're these long silver things with blades the size of dinner plates. When they see the real thing—which tends to be short, light, and pretty dinged up after a thousand years—they usually say something like "Huh," or "Wow, they're so small," and then move on to the display of fancy replica swords.

Which is exactly what just happened with the group I'm guiding around the museum.

A man in a polo shirt points at the row of longswords behind glass. "So, which are replicas and which are real?"

I put on the smile Grandpa always wears on the museum floor. The one that's warm but totally impersonal, like a borrowed hat. "All of those are replicas. Any ancient weapon will show a lot of corrosion. Like these." I point into the case of seaxes beside us.

The man gives them a glance. "Huh."

Like the battle axes, the seaxes aren't showy. They're angular, versatile blades with a single edge, about the length of a forearm. Women carried them as well as men. Poorer people used them. Farmers, shepherds. They were so common that a whole people was named after them. Saxons.

We have a couple of seaxes in our collection that date back several centuries, and one that's over a thousand years old. It's worn and dented, its wooden handle long since rotted away, leaving just a skinny metal stump. Looking at it, you wouldn't think: *Priceless*. But that shard of iron has been in the hands of actual Vikings. It's butchered deer, built longhouses, cleaved enemy bodies. It's hard to even imagine how many people have touched it as it's traveled through the centuries. And now this ancient seax is spending part of its life in a plexiglass box where tourists in golf shirts can say "Huh" at it.

"How much is one of these things worth?" the man asks, pointing toward the replica longswords again.

"It depends on the materials, the amount of time it took to make, who the smith is," I tell him, still wearing my borrowed-hat smile. "Lots of things."

The man doesn't really listen to my answer. He's nodding before I'm halfway done. He says something about gun collecting being a better investment to the guy beside him before swiveling toward the collection of spearheads.

"Let me know if you have any other questions," I say to their backs.

Then I head toward the front desk.

Les is there, in his usual button-up plaid shirt, sorting brochures at the register. He gives me a grin as I step closer. "How's it going, Frankie?"

"Fine. How's it going over here?"

"Quiet. Which is good. I'm asleep on my feet today."

The vision of Grandpa in the dark kitchen last night, the growl of the thunder, and the smells of ash and blood sweep through my brain. I whisk them out again. "Didn't get enough sleep last night?"

"Eh." Les looks away, rubbing the back of his scrawny neck with one hand. "If you want a good night's sleep, don't get old." He steps past me. "Got to grab that roll of tape from the storeroom."

I watch him cross the museum floor.

Suddenly Les's walk looks different to me. Or maybe it has looked like this for ages. Maybe I just haven't wanted to notice the stiffening, the way he holds his bony elbows out to either side, like hinges that are too rusty to bend.

Protect the people who belong here, no matter what comes.

"Hey," says a voice.

I jerk toward it.

And there he is, leaning on the other side of the counter.

The boy who *doesn't* belong here.

Max.

He's wearing a blue T-shirt this morning, with tiny holes along the shoulder seams and something printed across the front in a font that I can't read but that looks like it could have been spray-painted on a railroad car. Dark hair falls across his forehead.

"Hey." I lean away.

"How's it going?" His tone is light. I can't tell if he's really asking, or if this is just an empty piece of conversation, a habit. Because I don't know his habits. I don't know him.

"Fine," I answer.

"Pretty busy in here." He glances around. "I guess it's a good day to drive to a tiny town and learn about Vikings."

"I guess so."

Max draws back, taking his arm off the counter. "Sorry. I should have asked. Do I need to buy a ticket just to be in here?"

I frown. "You want to tour the museum again already?"

"No. I mean, to talk to you."

My heart does this weird thing where it feels like it's folding in half. It must be nervousness. Not excitement or anything. Because this is not a comfortable sensation.

I look over my shoulders, making sure Les is nowhere in earshot. Grandpa is out of sight in the office. Another feeling, something a little stronger than nervousness, presses on my heart.

"No," I say. "No, you don't have to. I mean, you can talk to me without . . . You can just talk."

"Okay." Max steps toward the counter. He's ignoring my awkwardness. I don't know if this is a kindness or if he doesn't perceive it in the first place.

"I've been cleaning out the fourth floor of the hotel," he goes on. "It's just unfinished attic space, but Ani's going to use it for storage or something. Anyway, it's full of old stuff, things that must have belonged to the hotel or to people who stayed in it over the years." He leans on the counter again. The way he moves, relaxed and comfortable even in a place where he doesn't fit, makes no sense to me at all.

"So, I've been going through this stuff," he says. "We'll probably just throw most of it away, but some of it is pretty cool. And I thought maybe somebody who's from here should look it over in case there's something significant. Somebody who knows this place. Who knows history." He stops, looking into my eyes.

"Somebody," I echo.

He grins now. "Yeah. Meaning you."

"So . . . you're asking me to come look through this stuff with you?"

"If you wouldn't mind."

I look down, away from his eyes. I notice the leather-and-bead bracelets still wrapped around his wrist. Maybe he never takes them off. Maybe he can't. There are spatters of black ink all over his fingertips. I realize I'm cataloging everything about him, like I'm Chuck or one of the other bird-watchers around here, noting all the characteristics of nonnative species.

"When you're free, I mean," Max says, because I still haven't answered. "Unless you don't want to."

"No," I hear myself say. "I want to."

And it's the truth. An attic full of hidden town history? Yes. I want to see that. And he's right: If there's something special there, something that belongs in this town, I don't want some outsider pawing through it. Throwing it away.

"I can be over in an hour or so," I tell him. "Duane will be here by then, so I can duck out."

"Cool." He smiles, backing away. "See you then."

He steps out the front doors.

I take a quick survey of the upper floor. No one else is nearby waiting to ask questions or offer to buy one of our horned helmets to wear to the next Vikings game. I slip out from behind the desk and around the corner to the office.

Grandpa is inside. I open the door quietly, so for a moment, I can see him as he is when he doesn't know he's being seen.

He's slumped in an office chair near the file cabinets. Even from the back, I spot stiffness. Pain. Pain in his posture, in the way he moves when he swivels around, closing the file cabinet behind him.

But the moment his eyes hit me, he smiles.

"Hey there," he says. "Need something? Les causing trouble?"

"Are you all right?" I ask at the same time, stepping closer.

Grandpa waves me back. "I'm fine. Just a little achy."

"You shouldn't have been out so late," I tell him. "Did you remember all your pills this morning?" I picture his pill box, as long as a ruler, lying on the kitchen counter, its pop-up lids hiding tablets of all colors and sizes.

He stops just short of rolling his eyes. "Yes, nurse. I took all my pills."

"Maybe you should go home and rest. I'll stay here this afternoon, in case Les or Duane needs any–"

Grandpa stands up. He straightens his shoulders, lifts his head, and he's my giant grandpa again, so tall that I have to look up when he steps closer. "Get out of here," he says, smiling, putting a hand on my shoulder. "You can help take care of this place, but it's not your job to take care of *me*. I don't pay you enough for that."

This is one of our old duets. I smile back at him. "You don't pay me at all."

"Exactly." Grandpa grins. "Go on now. I'll see you at home for supper."

I turn away, and the warmth of his big hand falls from my shoulder.

Of course Grandpa would tell me to go. Even if he needs me to stay.

I turn back again. "You sure I can't get you anything before I leave?"

"Oh, sure." Grandpa shrugs, still grinning. "You could get

me some of those self-organizing file cabinets. That would be great."

"I can help you with the filing tomorrow. I need to learn it all anyway." I stop, still a few steps from the door, and fold my arms across my chest. I want to look solid. Certain. Because I am.

"I've been thinking, Grandpa," I tell him. "About next year. After graduation."

Grandpa's eyes fix on me. He waits.

"I'm going to stay here."

Grandpa drops back down in his office chair. His face is carefully clear. "Here," he repeats.

"So I can help run the museum. Or not just help. I want to make it even better." The words rush out. "I have a lot of ideas. I want to add some special programs, maybe classes and presentations. Design a whole new website, increase our outreach. Get some more tourist money flowing into town. Maybe help some other local businesses stay open. Or reopen."

There's a sliver of a grin on Grandpa's face now. "You *have* been thinking."

"And if I want to, I can go to Winona or La Crosse part-time and live at home. Save money."

"Another good thought." Grandpa leans forward in the creaking chair. "But you know, your mom wants you to broaden your horizons. Get the whole college experience. I can't let this place"—he tips his head in a way that could mean the museum or the whole town—"be the thing that holds you back."

"Holds me back from what? Stuff I don't want?" I open my hands. "I *want* to be here. With you. In this place. It's my choice."

"Well." Grandpa gives a half nod. The grin is still there, restrained, almost hidden, but with joy and pride layered inside it. I know him well enough to see it all. "You've got time to think again, if you want to," he says. "But I'm not going to try to talk you out of anything."

"Don't bother," I tell him. "Stubbornness runs in my family."

Grandpa chuckles. I hear it behind me as I finally turn and head out the door.

April 5, 1986

Hey Matt,

I went out with some townies last night. And I mean literally went out, like out into the woods, because that's what they do here. They build a bonfire in a clearing somewhere, and then everybody stands around it, drinking beer, joking around, or just staring at the flames.

That's how I spent most of my night. Fire staring. I wasn't going to get drunk, for a bunch of reasons, but mostly because I don't want to mess up and forget part of my story. Like say I'm from Madison instead of Milwaukee, or call myself by the wrong last name, or blurt out any other stupid secrets.

So I just held my warm beer and stared.

No one cared that I was quiet anyway. I only got invited along kind of by accident. Bruce, this kid who makes deliveries to the hotel, was unloading stuff into the kitchen with me yesterday. It was all supposed to get stored downstairs, but the river water's so high that the basement of this old place is starting to leak, so now we all have to dodge around the crates while we're working. Bruce mentioned that he had an extra case of beer in his truck because people would be hanging out on the bluff just off Potter's Road. Then he said, "You could come," and went back to unloading. It was barely an invitation. It was more like a fact.

But blowing off a little steam sounded good. So I walked all the way up there after the supper rush at the hotel. (The truck's still screwed, obviously.)

People there were kind of weird. Just like at the hotel. They don't trust me because they don't know me, but they don't want to ask questions and actually GET to know me either.

I guess it doesn't matter. I can't let them know the real me anyway.

The whole thing was just kind of lonely.

Probably why I'm writing this long letter to you now. Ha ha.

Anyway, I got back to the hotel pretty late. It's weird. This place is DARK. Walking back down the bluff, through the streets, I realized that I'm not used to this much darkness. I'm used to streetlights, and signs, and light coming from somewhere, no matter how late it is. But this place is just . . . dark. While I was feeling my way along this little alley that leads to the kitchen door, which the Hanssons left unlocked for me, I looked up and realized how dark even the sky is around here. Because Black Point is miles and miles from a single city, even a small one. It's so dark you can see ten times as many stars as usual. So dark you can hear everything clearer too. I think I could even hear the river, extra high and fast right now, sloshing against the docks down on the other side of Main.

Anyway, I was already feeling weird when I got up to my room on the third floor. The rooms up here are that old-fashioned hotel style, where they all share one bathroom at the end of the hall. I headed down the hall to the bathroom. When I flicked on the bathroom light, I could see that the hallway carpet behind me was totally soaked with big wet footprints. I thought my shoes must have gotten wet out there in the woods, so I grabbed a towel and mopped them all up. Jeanne and Maeve have been great to me, and I'm not going to make them sorry for that if I can help it.

I went into the bathroom, did my thing, came back out. And the footprints were there again.

This time they didn't lead up to the bathroom door. They went down the hall in the opposite direction. But they didn't go into any of the rooms. Somewhere along the carpet, they just stopped.

I cleaned them all up again. Even though now I knew they weren't mine.

But here's the thing: I don't know whose they could have been.

Because there was no one else staying on the third floor last night.

Okay. Stay with me here, Matt.

There's a bunch of ghost stories about this place. I've heard bits of them, working here, stuff the townies said around the bonfire. Nothing special, just the kind of stories you hear about every old place.

But I'll admit it just to you, Matt. (AND YOU CAN STOP READING RIGHT HERE, ALICIA.)

This freaked me the hell out.

After I cleaned up the second footprints, I lay in my room with the door locked, listening to every little sound for I don't know how long.

Nothing happened, of course. I just gave myself a crappy night's sleep.

Still, I know what I saw. And those footprints were wet. Like, soaking wet. And I wasn't drunk, I swear, unless I can get drunk off three-fourths of one crappy beer an hour after drinking it.

In the daylight it all seems stupid. I'm not going

to run away screaming from a good job and room and board because of some dumb spots on a carpet. But I will feel a lot better once I've got enough money to fix the truck. Just so I know I CAN get out.

Hey, Matt. You can burn this letter too. Ha ha.

Your candy-ass brother,

Neil

5

I HEAD DOWN REDTAIL AND ALONG MAIN TOWARD THE HOTEL.

I feel self-conscious at first. Like anyone glancing at me out their car or store or house windows will know; like they'll be able to tell exactly where I'm going, who I'm going to see.

But that's ridiculous.

They'll just see me. And I belong here.

The town around me looks the same as always, except that the river is wider than usual, a wet spring and recent storms pushing its edges higher. Two big wooden posts that stand at either end of town mark the high points of past floods. The water's inching its way up the posts right now, toward 2001, when half the trees in Riverside Park pulled their roots out of the saturated mud and washed away. Toward 1952, when Black Point's original town hall was swamped for so long with water and rot that they had to tear it down. Toward 1965, the highest the water has ever been, when the river rose up and covered Main Street from side to side.

The Black Point Hotel has withstood them all.

Its heavy front doors swing open before I touch them.

Max stands in the doorway. Sounds pour out from around him: thumping and banging and whirring and shouting voices. "Hey," he says above the noise. "Come on in."

I step over the threshold. The big arched windows of the lobby are still covered with brittle brown paper, and the wooden bar still fills its wall—but everything else has shifted. The hanging red glass lamps have vanished, leaving bare bulbs behind like eyes without sockets. The tables and upturned chairs are piled in one corner, their legs sticking out as stiffly as the limbs of road-killed deer. A crew of builders is at work in the lobby, prying carpet from floorboards, hammering a hole through the kitchen wall. I don't recognize any of them. I don't recognize the woman standing near the bar either, the one talking into a cell phone, with thick dark hair pinned up on her head and pointed gold spikes dangling from her ears.

She gives me and Max a quick smile as he guides me past. She must be Ani. The aunt. The new owner.

"It's a lot quieter on the fourth floor," Max calls over his shoulder as we start up the staircase. "A lot stuffier too. I pre-apologize."

I glance at his back. There are traces of sweat on his shirt, a thin dark line down his spine, on the back of his collar. But he doesn't smell like sweat. When I inhale, I catch only deodorant and dust and warm skin.

I don't want to think about his warm skin.

We reach a landing. A long, narrow hall runs away from it, lined with rows of matching doors. The carpet is faded-blue paisley, the walls sand brown. Max leads me around a corner, up another switchback flight. The third-floor hall looks a lot like the second, but more faded. It is quieter up here. Almost silent. The air feels strange, too still, like something sealed up in a giant coffin.

Max leads the way down the narrow corridor. "Like I said before: mildewed."

Small brass numbers are tacked to each door we pass. 11. 12. 13. At the end of the hall, next to a door labeled Restroom, there's a nook, like an empty closet. Inside is a door to another set of stairs—narrow unfinished wooden ones. Our steps draw loud creaks from the planks.

"And here we are," says Max, stepping from the stairs into the room above.

That's what it is: one huge room with walls that tilt inward on each side, little juts in its layout formed by the points of the rooftops. The floor is bare boards. The air is muggy. Small, low windows line the walls.

I step toward one of them. I have to crouch to look through it, but from there I can see half the town stretching away below, the river sliding along beside it, forest and sloughs and marshes twisting into the distance. I've never seen it from this perspective, and somehow it makes the whole familiar place look different. Almost unrecognizable.

Max heads toward a heap of objects: spilling trunks, old boxes, broken lamps, and seatless chairs.

"This is the stuff I've been sorting through," he says. "Some of it is really old. Like, not Viking-era old, but *old*. Here—like this."

He pushes one box between us, and we both crouch beside it. Max lifts out a camera. A square heavy one, maybe from the 1950s. There's an old pair of binoculars, some books on birds and wildflowers, notebooks full of scribbled words about Midwestern wildlife. A hand-knit yellow sweater full of moth holes. There are no names anywhere, not inside the books or notebooks. Nothing that I recognize.

"Hmm," I say. "I guess someone might want some of this. The camera anyway."

"There's no film in it anymore. I checked. But that would have been cool." He nudges the other boxes with his foot. "There's some more interesting stuff in these."

I pass over a crate piled with bedding and open another cardboard box. This one is full of slightly newer things: a stained T-shirt, a Stephen King paperback, a pair of stonewashed jeans.

Max grasps something from a rack of hanging clothes. "This is what I really wanted to show you."

The long, pale thing draped over his arm swishes through

the dusty air as he turns back to me, almost like it's moving on its own.

It's a wedding dress.

A really old one. It's made of ivory fabric, with a long skirt, layers of lace, and rows of tiny buttons running up its bodice. I step closer, close enough that I can see the threads along the collar that are starting to break and tangle together like the edges of an old cobweb. I touch its sleeve. It's soft and cool, even up here in the attic's dusty heat.

"Remember the ghost you told me about?" Max looks from my face to the dress. "The woman in white?"

Of course, that's where my mind has gone too. But I pull it back.

I'm not sure why. Maybe because if Max is right, that would make him a part of the story. And he's not a part of it. The story is ours.

"Or maybe it's just Jeanne Hansson's old wedding dress," I say.

Max frowns slightly. "She's the one who used to run this place?"

"Yeah, she and her daughter, Maeve. Jeanne died, like, thirty years ago."

"Was she a hundred and fifty? Because this thing looks *really* old."

I do the math. Maeve is a little younger than Grandpa and the Oldies. She must have been born in the 1950s. So her mother probably *didn't* wear a wedding dress that looks like it could have gone to a party for Queen Victoria.

I drop the edge of the sleeve. "Then someone left it behind. People leave all kinds of things in hotel rooms."

"But who leaves a wedding dress behind? Unless *they* never leave either?" Max's tone is almost playful. Like he's doing the voice-over for a scary movie and mocking it at the same time.

"That's another thing I wanted to tell you about," he goes on, hanging the dress on its rack again. "There's a lot of mismatched junk here, like single socks, and old books and hats and whatever. But I think there are *sets* of stuff, too. Like entire boxes that belonged to one person. There's that box with the camera and binoculars and bird-watching books." He kicks another carton. "This one has romance novels, and a jacket and shoes, and a purse full of stuff. No wallet, but a bunch of jewelry, five kinds of lipstick, a gold lighter. It's not like someone just forgot something. It's like they left *all* their things behind. It's weird."

I'm not going to let the sharpness in his eyes hook mine. "Maybe they were in a hurry. Maybe they were running off without paying their bill."

One of Max's eyebrows goes up. "Like dine and ditch? Sleep and scram?"

"Maybe." The eyebrow annoys me. "I don't know what they call it in Minneapolis."

One corner of his mouth goes up too. "Oh yeah. We sleep and scram all the time."

"You should just go and ask Maeve about this stuff." I turn away from him and his almost-smile. "She runs that little shop on Main Street. I'm sure there's an explanation. Probably the same one I already gave you."

He nods, skimming the boxes with his eyes again. "So, nothing you want for the museum, then?"

I finally look straight at him. "No. No priceless historical objects here."

"Well, damn." He grins back. Then he bends, tossing a few spilled books back into an open crate. His fingers are still splotched with black.

"What did you do to your hands?" I can't help asking.

He glances down. "Oh. Exploding ink pen."

"Like—some kind of prank thing?"

"No, like cheap art supplies. I draw," he says, meeting my eyes. "Kind of."

I don't know why I ask the next question. Maybe it's because I'm somewhere I've never been, with someone I don't really know, and everything seems half unreal anyway.

"Can I see?"

Minutes later we're downstairs on the second floor, inside the room where Max is living. It's eerily close to what I pictured. Single bed, faded wallpaper, wood-framed landscape art on the walls, plus an explosion of stuff that I hadn't pictured scattered on top of it all: cords and headphones and T-shirts and books and empty aluminum cans and paper and markers.

I hadn't meant to invite myself into his room. Not exactly.

I hover in the doorway, wanting to step inside and examine

everything, tug open the drawers, stare out the window and see if I can spot my own house from here. But I keep still.

Max steps to the tiny desk against one wall. There's a rotary phone on its corner next to a glass ashtray and a squat brass reading lamp. He picks up a sketchbook and hands it to me.

I still can't read his expression. It could be modesty, or false modesty, or confidence, or nothing. I open the sketchbook instead.

"Oh," I say out loud, before I mean to. Because he's good.

Really good.

There are all kinds of things on the pages. People, buildings, trees, eyes, hands, creatures that are real and some that aren't. Some are done in pencil, some are finished in black ink. His style is vaguely like something you'd see in a comic book—a weird comic book—or in a collection of creepy folklore. But all of them are really, really good.

"Are you studying art in school?" I ask him.

Max laughs. He leans against the front of the desk, inky hands on its edge. "No. I've got one more year of high school. Then I'll probably study graphic design or something. As much as I like drawing, I also really like food. I'd like to keep eating it." He shrugs one shoulder. "I'll keep sketching, probably. Like a zillion other people who wish Alan Moore would show up at their door and ask them to illustrate his next graphic novel." He looks at me. "What about you? Or—are you already out of high school? I have no idea how old you are."

"I'll be seventeen on Monday."

"So this will be your senior year too?"

"Yeah." I close the sketchbook. I would keep looking through it, but it's starting to feel strange with him so close by. It feels more and more like I'm staring at *him*. I pass it back.

"What are you going to do afterward?" he asks, taking it.

"Run the museum," I answer.

He looks surprised—either by the speed of my answer or the answer itself.

"Really?" he says. "Wow. So—you'll stay right here?"

I stare back at him. The certainty I'd felt just an hour ago, standing in the museum office, telling Grandpa my plans, gives a sudden waver. I don't like it. "Is that strange?"

"No. It's not, I guess." But his eyebrows stay up. "It just seems like a huge job."

"It *is* a huge job," I say. "My grandpa and his friends aren't getting younger. Someone needs to take it over, and do it right, or it will all disappear."

"Is that what you want to do?" He lays out the words. "Run a museum?"

"It's exactly what I want to do." My voice is growing sharper. "It's how I've spent my whole life. Why do you think I wouldn't want to?"

He shrugs. "I don't know. Most people want to go somewhere else. See something else, do something else. At least for a while. Instead of just staying in one little place."

"Most people." I repeat his words. "Most people are idiots. Thinking they have to want what everybody else wants. Thinking they have to leave a place they know and care about, so they can move to some other place they *don't* know and *don't* care about, where they'll just pack up and leave again and never really be part of anything at all." Now my voice is a blade. "How do you think anything survives? How is anything supposed to last if nobody holds on to it? If they just let other people come in and rip it up, tear it down, turn it into a *bistro* or a *cidery* or whatever, and when that fails, someone else will come in and tear it down all over again?"

I finally stop, glancing at Max's face. He's watching me with his gold-brown eyes. Just watching. Listening. With that impossible-to-read expression back in place.

I step backward. The ancient floor creaks under my heel.

"I should go," I tell him. "And all that stuff in the attic . . . you can just throw it away."

I turn and bolt down the staircase, through the sawdust and roar of the lobby, out into the light.

April 7, 1986

Hey Matt,

Well, I went over to Swede's Garage this morning and talked to the guys about the truck. One of them's a regular at the hotel, so he knows me a little. Enough not to pick my pockets, I hope. They sent a tow for the truck, so now it's sitting in the lot full of other rustbuckets until I can get some cash together. Parts and labor shouldn't be too bad. But still, until Jeanne pays me next week, I've got $1.50 to my fake name.

I mean, I've got a good thing going here. I'm not going to run away because of a wet carpet. I just want to know I CAN.

Besides, the next day, after that bonfire and the weird stuff back at the hotel, everything seemed pretty normal. I worked the Sunday lunch and dinner shifts, Jeanne made meatballs, and Maeve baked her apple cake, which is so good it makes you want to climb up on the bar and tap dance.

Not that anybody did that. All anybody is doing is talking about how high the river is, that it's already covered the railroad tracks and a bunch of buildings at the bottom of the hill—like the hotel—are flooding already, and arguing about whether it's going to get any higher.

I overhear enough in the bar to pick up all this. Even though I'm not FROM here. Like everyone keeps reminding me.

Jeanne and Maeve are so nice, though, it makes up for a lot of the rest. They even make my bed if I forget to do it myself. It's kind of like having a mom looking out for you. Remember what that was like?

Pretty great.

Maeve could tell something was going on with me yesterday. Maybe it's because she's "psychic." Or maybe I was wearing it on my face. Anyway, she stopped me while I was carrying a tub of dishes to the kitchen sink, and she stared straight into my eyes for a second. And then she said, "You saw something, didn't you?"

I kind of pretended not to know what she was talking about. I didn't want *to know what she was talking about. But I guess she saw through me, because next she said, "Which ghost was it?"*

I said, "There's more than one?"

She smiled this creepy little smile and said that this place is really old, and the past is soaked straight into it, but that the ghosts probably don't mean me any harm.

It was all so screwy. I put down the dishes, and

I said I was fine, but that I might be heading on in another week or so, once the truck was running and I'd saved up a bit. And she said, really quietly, "That might be best for you."

Just the way she said it, all whispery, with those weird eyes . . . Man, it gave me goose bumps.

So I finished my shift, and I went up to bed, even though Jeanne and a bunch of other old timers were still sitting up in the bar talking about how bad the flooding got ten years ago, or twenty years ago, or whatever.

I slept with the door chained shut and the reading lamp on. Because I'm a wimpy little baby. There, I said it for you. Ha ha.

When I woke up in the morning, everything seemed fine. Then I swung my bare feet out of bed and stepped straight into a puddle. Feel free to make a joke about me wetting the bed right here, Matt.

I knew I hadn't spilled anything on the carpet. Plus, it smelled like dirty water, not like anything else. I checked the ceiling for leaks, but there weren't any. And when I opened the blinds, I saw it wasn't just one puddle. There were a bunch of them. They were spaced out, like footprints. They led from the door straight to my bed.

But the door was still locked. Chained shut.

From the inside.

There's no way anyone could have gotten in. Right? Right.

So now what do I do? Do I tell crazy Maeve about it? Do I tell Jeanne and look like I'M the crazy one? Do I ask some of the townies about this stuff and hope they'll actually talk to me?

I don't know.

Man, I wish you were here right now, Matt.

I'd call you, but I know dad could pick up instead. I don't have money for long-distance calls anyway. And I sure as hell can't call collect.

I guess what I should do is buck up and stop being a (excuse my French, Alicia) chickenshit.

Right? Right.

See, I can just talk to myself.

Okay. I'll write more soon.

–Neil

6

ON MY BIRTHDAY MORNING, THREE ENVELOPES WAIT FOR ME on the breakfast table.

One is white, with just my name written on the outside, so I don't know who it's from. One is from Grandma Molitor, who I haven't seen since I was little, but who sends a card every year. And one is from my dad.

My parents divorced when I was three. Mom and Dad met at college in Winona, and then Mom convinced my dad to move to Black Point for a while, but she says he didn't like it here. The town never really warmed up to him either—it's hard to welcome someone who makes it clear that they don't want to be there in the first place. And when my dad suggested other, faraway places, Mom wouldn't go. Her mother was sick, and I was little, and she already had a good job at the library, and when she weighed everything in Black Point against my dad,

Black Point won. So my dad left. He lives in California now, in a house I've never seen, with a wife I've never met. I've been invited to visit. I'm just not interested. His life seems about as real to me as a page torn from a magazine.

I wonder if Mom always knew things with him were temporary. She gave me her family name, not his. She chose to live here, not anywhere else. She never even moved most of her stuff out of the big house up on Fourth down to the little house she and Dad rented on Second Street. When I was old enough to ask her about it, Mom told me she and Dad were never right for each other, but she got me, so everything turned out exactly the way it was meant to be.

I think she's right.

I have everyone and everything I need right here.

I rip open Dad's card. The envelope is pale blue, and the card inside has glittery balloons, forty dollars in cash, and a note saying he'll call soon. Grandma Molitor's is almost identical, except the envelope is purple and there's no promise to call.

"Happy birthday, sweetheart," says Mom, bustling into the kitchen. She bends over the table to kiss my head.

I smile up at her. "Thanks."

"I've got a full day, but you and Grandpa and I will celebrate tonight. You're not working at the museum today, are you?"

"Nope." I squish a muffin crumb on my plate. "Grandpa insisted I take the day off."

"Good. Well, have a lovely one. Do something fun. Just make

sure you're out of the house between five and five-thirty."

I give her a skeptical look. "Mom . . ."

"No arguments, Lucia." She smiles brightly back at me. "There just *might* be a couple of items we want to bring into the house without you watching." She grabs her bag. "See you then."

The kitchen door whooshes shut. Out the front windows I can see Mom hurrying down the shady sidewalk to the library.

I pick up the third envelope. Someone local must have put it in our mailbox. Maybe a neighbor, or Cara or Bailey, or one of the Oldies. Although I don't recognize the handwriting.

I rip it open. Inside is one folded page, and on it is a drawing of an armored valkyrie with a shield and spear standing amid a pile of bodies. It takes me a few seconds to realize that all the bodies are dressed in Minnesota Vikings paraphernalia. And it takes me a few more seconds to realize that the valkyrie looks like me. My straight, light-blond hair. My long nose. My jaw. She's even got a tiny Viking Museum of Black Point badge on her chest.

I smile, even though nobody's there to see it.

I put the birthday money and the drawing in my jeans pocket. Then I head down Fourth Street to Falcon Avenue, straight up to the front doors of the old hotel.

Ani appears between the double doors when I knock. She's wearing another black shirt and another pair of dangling gold earrings, and her phone is pinned between her shoulder and her ear. "Sorry," she murmurs. "Leaking basement. I'm on hold with the contractor. Are you looking for Max?" She waves me inside.

"He's painting in there," she adds, pointing to the back corner of the lobby before striding away.

The swinging wooden door marked Ladies' Room is wedged open. Inside, behind two wooden stalls, I find Max standing on a ladder, painting the walls eggshell white. Scraps of wallpaper litter the floor like wilted petals.

As I inch into his vision, Max turns. He looks surprised to see me. But not *too* surprised. It's just a quick shift in his face, a blink, then a smile. It's familiar enough to me now that I can tell the smile is genuine.

"Hey," he says, lowering a paint roller. "Happy birthday."

"Thank you." I put my hands in my pockets. "And thanks for the drawing. Do you need it back, or—"

"No," he says quickly. "It's for you."

I run my fingers over the folded paper. Then I pull my hand out of my pocket and leave the drawing there, pressed against my hip.

Max dips the roller into its tray. Freckles of white paint dot his hands, overlapping the ink stains that still cling there. "So, how are you spending your birthday?"

"My family is having a special dinner. I guess there's a secret gift on the way."

"You're not working at the museum?"

"Compulsory day off."

He gestures toward a brush on the paper-covered countertop. "Want to spend it helping paint a bathroom?"

"Sounds great," I say. Because having something to do with my hands is just what I need. I swipe the brush through the paint tray and run it across the lower wall.

Seconds slide by.

"I need to apologize to you," I say at last, looking at the wall instead of at Max. "I shouldn't have blown up like that yesterday."

"I'm just glad you weren't holding a battle axe at the time," he says. "Although I suppose you could do some damage with a paintbrush."

I laugh a little, but I don't look up. "No. I mean it. I got defensive and weird, because it's already this big thing. My mom wants me to go away to college. My best friends are going to leave. My teachers are pushing me. But I can see what's happening with my grandpa. And with this town." I swallow. "I need to be here. I *want* to be. So I can try to hold on to everything." I streak more white paint across the plaster. "That's why I flipped out. It wasn't you. And I'm sorry."

"*I'm* sorry," he says. "It's your life. Your choice." He dips the roller. The room gets brighter with each stripe.

"I think you're lucky," Max goes on, after a beat. "My family has moved a lot. Extended family, I mean. To New York, to Minnesota, and then some to California, and some back to Minnesota, and then some others from New York to Chicago and then to wherever. So there's no place that feels like *the* place, you know? It must be nice to have deep roots somewhere."

Deep roots, I think. The kind that can't be disturbed, or the tree will fall. No matter how big and sturdy it looks.

I make another streak of eggshell white.

"When I'm done with this wall, I'm free for the day." Max looks down at me. "I was actually thinking about going over to Maeve's store, like you suggested, and asking her about the stuff in the attic. Want to come along?"

"Sure," I say.

Because I do. Because it feels right: doing something different, with someone who only knows me right now, who has never called me "Frankie," who doesn't know the Lucia Sorenson that I've been ever since I was born here seventeen years ago. It feels like a birthday.

I glance up at Max from the corner of my eye. The choppy dark hair. The leather bands on his wrists. I wonder what he notices when he looks at me. I wonder, if you took away this place and my past in it, what would be left to see. Just the thought feels wide open and a little scary, like a free fall. A rush of cool air.

An hour or so later Max and I head down Main Street. The sky is vivid blue, turning the surface of the river to a melted, wavery mirror. Sunlight slices the shadows beneath every tree. Whiffs of water and mud and frying dough from the bakery braid together around us.

At first, I walk ahead of Max, which makes him walk faster to keep up. As we march past the gas station and Swede's Garage, going so fast now that we both have to lean forward to keep our balance, I realize why I'm doing this.

I'm afraid someone will see us side by side.

Of course someone will see us. Every business we walk past, every truck that drives by has someone who knows me inside it. I can't walk fast enough to outrun this.

So finally I slow down to a normal human pace. Max catches up with me. He gives me one quick glance, and there might be a smile on his face, but it's gone again before I can read it.

"Where's this shop?" he asks.

"One more block."

"And it's a gift shop?"

"That's what it says on the door. It's really more of a junk store, art gallery, new age–weirdness shop. I'm guessing it's a lot like the inside of Maeve's mind. Everybody says she's *psychic*, but she's probably just . . ." I shrug. "Well. You'll see." I point ahead. "Her store's right there."

In the row of weathered wood and brick buildings that lines this part of Main Street, Maeve's place stands out like a parakeet in a row of sparrows. It's painted seafoam green, with tattered prayer flags and ribbons strung across its facade, and heaps of sun-bleached synthetic flowers spilling from its window boxes. The big plate glass window in front is painted with Black Point Gifts–Art, Treasures, Natural Wonders.

I push open the door for both of us.

I haven't stepped into Maeve's shop in years, and either the smell is stronger than I remember, or it's gotten worse. It's the smell of too much incense, old books, and an uncleaned litter box. The air is only slightly cooler than outside. It hangs around us like fog.

The main room of the shop is basically impossible to see. It's too full of stuff to make out its colors or dimensions at all. There are shelves of pulpy used paperbacks, hanging quilts and beaded dream catchers, mobiles made of car parts and driftwood. Bundles of sage. Pine cone wreaths. A scuffed glass counter fills one side of the room, its interior crammed with stones: glazed crystals, agates, pebbles from the river. Between the stones are decks of tarot cards, dried flowers, a confused rainbow of incense cones.

There's no one else inside.

"Whoa," says Max. I watch his face as he gazes around, nodding to himself. Then he turns to me, and there's a tiny smile around his mouth. "While we're here, we should really pick out a birthday present for you. Something useful."

"Yes." I nod back. "This place is full of things I need."

"That *everyone* needs." Max points at a wind chime made of bent silverware.

There's a rustling sound from behind me.

Max and I both turn.

Maeve Hansson steps through a hanging silk curtain into the space behind the counter.

She's a big woman, pale skinned and pale eyed. Her thick hair is lightening from straw to white. She might be made of snow or milk glass, just infinitely sturdier.

She gives me a long look. "Frank's girl. Lucia," she says, pronouncing each syllable heavily. *Lu-see-ah.* "Haven't seen you in a while."

"Yeah," I answer, putting a little space between myself and Max. "How are you, Maeve?"

She doesn't answer. Her eyes gaze past me, frozen on Max.

"You must be Ani's nephew," she says.

Maeve wouldn't have needed any psychic gifts to put this together. Boys who look like Max don't show up in Black Point every day.

Max looks like he's figured this out too.

"Right. I'm Max," he says, stepping toward the counter. "Nice to meet you."

Maeve doesn't reply.

"Everybody was surprised that you'd sold the place," I cut in. "We thought you never would."

Maeve's eyes float to me. "It was finally the right time," she says. Her eyes shift back to Max. "Lots to do, to get that place going again."

"Yeah," Max answers. "We're fixing things up, clearing things out." He takes another step toward the counter. "That's why we stopped in, actually. I've been going through the stuff in the attic, all those boxes, the things from different eras."

He stops, looking at Maeve.

I do too. Maeve doesn't shift, doesn't speak. Her eyes are like an overcast sky: gray-blue, hazy, any glimpse of sun or moon or stars hidden underneath.

"So, I'm sorting through everything, and I'm wondering about some of the stuff that I found." Max pulls his phone from his pocket. "I mean, some of it seems like it might be important to someone. And we figured you would know what the stuff is, at least."

"Old things," says Maeve dismissively. And vaguely. "Old things in an old place."

Max isn't letting go yet. He flips through the photos on his phone, stopping on a shot of something white and ruffled. "Like this. This dress." He turns the screen toward Maeve. Her eyes don't travel to it. "I've heard the stories about the woman in white," Max continues. "Maybe it's crazy, but I was just wondering if this was where it all started. If this was her dress."

"Yes," says Maeve simply.

"Yes?" Max leans on the counter, like he can't quite trust his ears.

But I heard it too.

"So—this was her wedding dress?" Max goes on. "And she died? At the hotel?"

"People die everywhere," says Maeve.

"Sure," says Max. "But *she* died *here*? Do you know her real name? Anything else about her?"

"It was a long time ago."

And I guess that's an answer. Sort of.

"Okay," says Max, after a beat. "There are some other things I noticed. Like there are some boxes full of things that look like they all belonged to one person." He shows Maeve another photo, then another. From the side, I can see the yellow sweater and camera and bird-watching books, the stonewashed jeans and paperbacks, the purse and the jewelry and the old tubes of lipstick.

"We were just wondering . . ." Max looks over at me. For support, I suppose. But I'm not quite ready to be part of this *we*. I look down at a tray of crystals and keep quiet.

"I was wondering," Max amends, "why somebody would stay at a hotel and leave all their stuff behind. Especially valuable stuff. Like their jewelry. Their wedding dress."

"People don't need the things they think they need," says Maeve, her gaze sliding across his phone and away again. "Enough time, enough people, everything gets left behind."

"But these *specific* people," Max says. "Do you know who they are? Or who they were? Why they left this stuff behind? If someone's out there who would want it back?"

"You can know who someone is without knowing who they are." Maeve pauses. Her eyes travel to me, heavy and chilly as snowdrifts. "Hotels and flowerpots have a lot in common," she goes on at last, turning back to Max. "Things live in them without putting any roots in the ground. Then, when they're gone, they're just *gone*. No traces."

Now Max looks as if he'd like to smack his face into the glass counter. I push back a laugh and break in.

"So you *do* know who these people were?" I ask Maeve. "Like, you know their names?"

"You know how many people check in to hotels under false names?" Maeve says back.

Which is a clearer answer than most of them have been.

"But if the wedding dress belonged to somebody who died here a long time ago, like the woman in white," says Max, "did these other things belong to other people who—who *died* there, too?"

Finally, Maeve seems to sharpen. Her eyes focus on the phone that Max is still holding out. "Can't say for sure," she answers. "It was all a long time ago. I wasn't there for most of it. It's an old place. The hotel. The town." She looks at Max again. "You should throw it all out. Or keep it up there forever. It doesn't matter. The things don't matter, either way."

Then her eyes flash to me, and for a second, I see stars through the clouds. "You're a Gemini," she says. "Late June birthday."

I don't know if she's *seeing* this or remembering it. Either one is surprising.

"Um—yeah," I stammer. "It's today, actually."

"I'm going to give you something," Maeve says. She nods toward Max. "But it's really for him."

She pulls a tray of stones out of the counter. She drops one little black crystal and a slip of paper inscribed with a rune into a tiny cloth bag. She pulls the drawstring and hands the bag to Max.

"Protection," she says.

"You mean . . . against the ghosts?" asks Max, and I can tell that he's trying to look solemn. Like all of this is totally sensible.

"Oh, no," says Maeve, as though the question is silly. "They're no threat to you. But the water's getting high. You'll want to be careful. Both of you." She glances toward me for a second, then back at Max.

We all waver there, caught in a quiet beat, until a huge orange cat leaps out from behind the silk curtain and onto the glass counter, asking, "Mrrr?" Max and I take a little step back.

"Okay," says Max, like the cat just woke him up. "Well—thanks. For the charm. And the talk."

"You're welcome," says Maeve distractedly. She has turned away from us, toward a rack above the counter, rearranging a few dangling suncatchers on strings.

"Bye, Maeve," I add as we head out the door.

For a second, Max and I just stand on the sidewalk of Main Street, blinking around at the bright, clear afternoon.

"So that's Maeve," says Max at last.

"Yeah," I answer. "And yes, she's always like that."

"I think I'm more confused than when we went in."

"Being around Maeve will do that. It's like jumping on and off a merry-go-round."

"So," says Max again, rubbing one hand through his choppy dark hair. "There are old things, but things don't matter. Ghosts exist. But we shouldn't worry about them. We should worry about the high water instead. And I should throw that stuff away and forget it and also keep it forever. Did I get everything?"

"I think so." I point at the little bag in his hand. "Oh, and don't forget about *that* thing, which she gave *you* because it's *my* birthday."

Max laughs, and I do too.

"Time well spent," he says, shoving the bag into his pocket. "Damn," he adds. "We forgot to get something for you."

I wave a hand. "It's okay. I've got all the magic rocks I need."

"What if I bought you lunch, then?"

"Lunch?" I echo. My brain slides out of this conversation and into one of the booths at Lou's, where every other person inside—Grandpa's friends, our neighbors, Lou herself—is staring at me, wondering what I'm doing sitting across from this boy with the bracelets and long hair and ink on his hands.

No.

I need to get him away from downtown. Away from every business and window and car. Out into the woods. For some reason, the thought of getting away from *him* doesn't even cross my mind.

"Let's just grab something at the gas station and then go for a walk," I say quickly. "I can show you something else. If you're—if you're still free, I mean. And if you're not too scared of the high water."

He looks at me for a half second. Then he starts to smile again. "Yeah. I'm free."

April 9, 1986

Hey Matt,

Bet you're dying for another shot of small-town drama. Am I right?

Here goes: The river keeps getting higher and higher. It's happening gradually enough that it doesn't seem like a big deal, but then you notice that it's already swamping places all along the edge of town. Last night, this big old ballroom and banquet hall, the kind of place where everybody around here has their wedding receptions and graduation parties, collapsed into the water. By morning every trace of it was gone. So everybody's all upset about that.

Everybody but me, I suppose. I've got other stuff to worry about.

I haven't seen any more of those weird wet footprints, but I have gotten up the last two mornings and found that my door was unlocked. I mean, the chain on the inside was still in place, because I always sleep with the chain on now, and it doesn't look like anyone has gotten in or anything. But I don't know how the knob keeps getting unlocked. Plus, once, I found a cigarette butt with a smudge of pink lipstick on it in the ashtray in my room.

You know I don't smoke, Matt. And no, I haven't started wearing lipstick, either.

Maeve doesn't smoke. Jeanne does, but she doesn't wear lipstick, not that I've ever seen. And even if it was one of them, why would they have gone into my locked room, smoked a cigarette, and left it behind? But if it wasn't one of them, who the hell else could it be?

I was going to bring all this up with Jeanne, ask if maybe my doorknob was broken and we could replace it or something. But things are kind of weird with her now, too.

Yesterday, after lunch, when the bar was totally empty except for Jeanne doing receipts and me gluing new felt pads on a chair, some guy came in. I could tell he wasn't from here, because I'd never seen him before, and he was wearing a blazer, and Jeanne said, "What can I do for you?" She usually doesn't need to ask.

The man went up close to the register and talked to her. The place was quiet enough that I caught most of what he said. Turns out he was a private investigator. He'd been hired to try to find a missing woman named Carol or Cheryl or something who had been passing through this area when she disappeared about twenty years ago. He said the police had no leads, the case had gone cold, and a bunch of other things you'd hear on Columbo. He showed Jeanne some pictures, and he asked some questions about dates and hotel records and stuff. Jeanne mostly just shook her head and said "sorry" over and over. Then the guy left her his card and headed out again.

Jeanne looked over at me. It was pretty obvious I'd overheard the whole thing.

"You know how many thousands of people have stayed here in my lifetime?" she said. "And I'm supposed to remember somebody from twenty years ago?"

Then she laughed a little, so I did too.

But the rest of the night, I swear, she acted different. Looking at me more than usual, her eyes all sharp. I don't know if the PI freaked her out or if it was something else, like if there were rumors going around about me, if somebody had figured out I've been using a fake last name or whatever. But she didn't say anything.

So the next day I tracked down that townie Bruce Larson while he was making deliveries at the bar up the block. I asked him if people would be hanging out in the woods again anytime soon. And he said yeah, they were going to be meeting up the next night, just off a road north of town where the water wouldn't be too high.

And I went along. Because I wanted to hear more of the hotel ghost stories, and I figured a bunch of drunk townies my own age were more likely to talk than a bunch of old townies whose tolerance is way higher.

We all stood around a bonfire out there, me and six other guys. I waited until they were all a few beers deep, and then I said something like, "Hey, you all remember the stuff you told me about the hotel being haunted?" And that was all it took. So at least one thing went my way.

Get this, Matt. There's not just a ghost called the woman in white, who's a bride who died on what was supposed to be her wedding day. There's some dead bootlegger who loves jazz music. There's a ghost they call the lipstick lady, who leaves lipstick smudges on cigarettes and pillowcases when no one is around. And there's the drowned man, who tracks wet footprints through empty rooms.

Dude. I had to clench my entire body to keep from pissing myself.

I asked something like, "Does anybody know how they died? Why they'd still be hanging around?"

They said the bride had killed herself by taking poison or something, more than a hundred years ago. The bootlegger supposedly got whacked by Al Capone. One skinny totally wasted kid spewed out the whole story about the drowned man: He was a bird-watcher or nature writer or something, and he'd come here back in the fifties to study the wildlife along the river, and then he'd drowned in the bottoms and never been found. (I don't know how they know you've drowned if your body is never found, but it's pretty pointless to talk logic with someone as plastered as this kid.) Then some guy in head-to-toe camo broke in about the lipstick lady. She was running away from a husband or boyfriend in Chicago, and possibly she'd stolen a bunch of money too, and she came here to hide out but then disappeared. "He probably caught up with her," the guy finished. "Dumped her body somewhere out here."

By this point I was starting to think they were messing with me. Trying to freak me out or scare me off. See if they could make me piss my pants after all.

I said something about how that was an awful lot of people to "disappear" from one tiny little town. How it's kind of crazy that all these people could just vanish.

That skinny wasted kid said something like, ". . . It's the water." And then he puked on Bruce's boots.

It started to rain right after that. We all got out of there, headed back to town before the mud could get any muddier, so I didn't get to ask any more questions. It doesn't matter anyway. I'm not going to stick around here much longer. I mean, I don't believe in this ghost stuff, not one hundred percent, but I'd rather be someplace without weird lipstick stains and wet footprints showing up in my room either way.

Even if I wait another week or two, I don't know how much money I'll have left over after I cover the truck repairs. And I might not be lucky enough to find another steady job so fast. So—

Damn, I hate even writing this.

Maybe you could send me a little cash, Matt? Whatever you can spare. Even twenty bucks would be a big help. I'll pay you back when I can. I swear. Just like I swear I'll return your tapes.

If you can, just mail the money to the hotel. Remember, I'm Neil SCHMIDT here. It's 121 Main Street, Black Point, Wisconsin.

Make sure no one knows you're doing it.

Thanks, Matt.

Let's hope the ghosts don't get me in the meantime.

Ha ha.

—Neil

7

HALF AN HOUR AFTER LEAVING MAEVE'S SHOP, MAX AND I are walking along the curve of County H, just north of the edge of town. It's quiet. As soon as you turn off the River Road and into the bottoms, the world hushes so suddenly, it's like you've closed a door behind you. The earth dips down, and the trees thicken, and in less than a quarter mile, there's no sign of cars or houses or anything else that means you're not alone.

The high water turns the forest floor into a marsh. Pools seep between the trees, reflecting the trunks and high green branches that reach down into a second sky under our feet. You have to know where to step, or you can lose a shoe in the thick mud or plunge straight into waist-deep water.

Fortunately, I know where to step.

"Here's the turn," I tell Max, leading the way onto a ridge that will keep us on higher ground, winding up through the trees.

"The turn to what?" asks Max. "Some axe murderer's isolated cabin?"

"You'll see," I tell him, grinning over my shoulder.

The ridge wends through a stretch of old forest. Around us, thin streams trail through strips of grassy land, connecting ponds to marshes to more streams, all eventually heading back to the river itself. Everything is as green as an emerald and as soft as mist.

Birds trill. Wind shuffles the leaves on the ashes and willows.

"This way," I say, leaving the ridge now. I hop over one rivulet onto the next raised patch of land.

Max hops behind me, lands a step short, and ends up with one foot in the water.

He gives a stagey gasp. "Oh my god—Maeve told us to watch out for high water. She *is* psychic."

I shake my head. "And that rock in a bag didn't even protect you."

"Last time I put my faith in a rock."

I smile and jump over another stream.

We head through a thick patch of box elder trees, down a slight slope, and here we are—at the edge of the Bend.

Founders' Bend is a sheltered spot, a place where the river curves inward and forms a bay, its edges surrounded by bluffs and trees. Reeds and willows encircle the waves. On one side the craggy face of the bluff—Black Point itself—plunges down to the water's lip, the rock as sharp and strong as sculpture. When the surface of the bay is still enough, the difference between water and air disappears, and it looks like an opening through the earth into another deeper, quieter world.

"Wow," says Max, very softly, from beside me.

And this is exactly the right thing to say.

Not that I'd been hoping for a specific response. But if he'd said anything else, it would have felt like a mistake, bringing him here.

It wasn't a mistake.

"See those gaps in the side of the bluff over there?" I say. "Those are caves. The one in the middle is big. Like, big enough for a bunch of people to get inside. That's where the four men who came from Sweden and founded the town took shelter for a year or two, before they started building houses and clearing land."

"Whoa," says Max. "Really? Can we go inside?"

"Probably not right now," I say. "The water's too high. When it's lower, there's a wide strip of land where you can walk right up to the cave openings. By late summer there's usually plenty of room."

I stop. What I've just said sounds almost like an invitation. Like an admission, or a hope, that he'll still be here in a few months.

"Do lots of people come out here then?" Max asks.

I shake my head. "Almost nobody knows about this place." I gaze past him, at the curtains of forest and walls of rock that enclose us, cutting us off from the rest of the world. "I mean—everybody knows that the founders sheltered in a cave for a while, but there are lots of caves in these bluffs. Most people don't know about this one. The Oldies like to keep it a secret. They don't want kids hanging out inside, getting drunk, spray painting their names on the walls. They want to honor it instead."

For a moment, we stand in the quiet. A breeze ripples through the willows. Across the pond, where a thinning line of trees separates us from the river's main artery, a blue heron lifts and soars away.

"I can see why somebody would want to stay here for good," says Max.

There's a flicker of motion in my chest, like another pair of beating wings.

Maybe he won't just leave in another few months. Maybe he won't be one more deserter.

Maybe my taking the leap of bringing him here wasn't a betrayal at all.

I'm not sure why I did it: leading a stranger out here, to this secret place. I've never brought anyone here before.

I've never wanted to.

Maybe that's my reason.

"To the old Norse people, certain spots in nature were sacred," I tell Max. In part because I want him to understand, and in part because I need to keep myself steady, to keep myself talking, to hold myself to things I know. "There would be specific lakes or hills or groves where they would worship, make offerings, communicate with the gods."

My mind skids back to that idiotic rainy night beside the bonfire. To the sheep's sticky blood pasting Jake's palm to mine. I flick those thoughts away.

I nod up at the sharp bluff towering over us, the clear water before us rippling with its reflection. "Anyway. That might have been why this spot felt right to the town founders. If it felt like one of those old sacred spaces." I pause. "Of course, it might have been sacred to someone *else* before they picked it, but they probably didn't think about that."

Max sits down on a grassy patch beside me, setting the full plastic bag from the gas station between us. He locks his arms loosely around his bent knees. "Do you believe in that?" he asks. "The sacredness of places?"

"Yeah." I sit down on the other side of the bag. "Definitely. I mean—I think something builds up when generations of people live in one spot. Memories. Stories. Spirits. The more things that have happened in one place, the more sort of *alive* it becomes."

Max tips his head to one side. "I guess I don't know what that's like at all. Generations in one place."

"Minneapolis doesn't feel sacred to you?"

He laughs. "It's got sacred spots, maybe. The Holy Uptown Theater. The Temple of First Ave. The Blessed Shrine of Spyhouse Coffee."

His tone is joking, but there's something in it, underneath, that's genuine. I turn to face him instead of the water.

I picture him in a busy coffee shop thronging with strangers. In the flickering dark of a theater. At a concert, surrounded by dancing nameless bodies, drumbeats echoing against the walls. I imagine what it would feel like to be there too. Somewhere new. With someone new. Everything new.

For a second, I want to reach over and touch him. I want to run my hand down his arm, lace my fingers between his and hold on.

But that's not going to happen. It can't. In no time at all, I'd have to let go.

I clench my own hands together as hard as I can. "Why did you really come here?" I ask.

He blinks, turning halfway toward me. "To help Ani."

"You didn't leave your sacred spots, and your stuff, and all your friends–I'm assuming you have friends–to come spend the summer in a tiny river town because you love stripping wallpaper."

His grin fades just a tiny bit. "Okay. Maybe my parents thought I should spend the summer being useful instead of lying around the house or hanging out with my friends. A.k.a. That Bunch of Losers."

"That's what your parents call them?" I ask. "Why?"

Max pulls a bottle of iced tea out of the bag. "We might have gotten into a little trouble because of some graffiti. And curfew issues. And a tiny bit of breaking and entering." He twists off the cap and takes a drink. ". . . And maybe disturbing the peace."

"Disturbing the peace how?"

"Maybe by playing the tuba in the street at two a.m."

I hear myself snort. "You play the tuba?"

"It wasn't my tuba."

I start to laugh. And then I can't stop. I keep picturing Max on a dark city street, cheeks puffed out, blatting away on a big brass tuba, and I laugh so hard my eyes blur.

Max watches me. He's grinning.

"What?" I ask, when I can finally stop.

"Nothing." He shrugs. "I like your laugh."

"Well. Thanks." I wipe my eyes. "I've had it forever."

He reaches into the bag again, pulls out the other bottle of iced tea, and hands it to me.

"What you were saying, about places and memories." Max sits up straighter now, bracing one elbow on his knee as he turns to me. "Do you think a place can have thoughts of its own? Like, it might want certain people in it? Or not?"

I look into his black-and-gold eyes. "Why? Are you feeling unwelcome here?" I wave an arm at the rustling grasses. "Or are you saying you've seen some hotel ghosts?"

His grin shifts. His gaze flicks away from mine. "No. Not like–I don't know. Maybe it's just memories, like you were saying. Whatever." He brushes a mosquito off his forearm before jumping to his feet. "Can we at least get a little closer to the cave? Even if we can't go inside?"

I hesitate.

The cave is secret. Sacred. Grandpa and the Oldies wouldn't want me bringing anyone else too close, especially someone who doesn't belong here in the first place.

But we won't be going inside, I remind myself. And the conversation that Max and I just had shows me that he understands. That he sees this place for what it is.

I get to my feet too, leaving the bag behind for now. "We can get closer. We'll just have to be careful."

I lead him onward over the marshy ground. The water is high enough that my usual path is gone, vanished under the muddy surface. But there's a second way, a little farther up the foot of the bluff. I take Max between the trees that cling to the rocks, their half-exposed roots like giant skeletal hands. We climb over and around their trunks, through the long grass, finally heading back downward toward the water.

The mouth of the cave looms lower and larger with each step I take. There's definitely no way inside right now. No *safe* way. The river nearly reaches the cave's bottom lip, and to get there, someone would have to wade or swim through the swollen water. Not a good idea when that water changes hour by hour.

I step down onto a wide rocky ledge, a strip of sandstone that juts from the earth like a blood vessel under skin. There are bare patches here, spots worn by other feet, other Black Point people—the few of us alive who know the way to this place.

Max moves past me, edging closer to the bluff. He climbs down from one broken boulder to another. Right below him another jut of rock presses up against the cave's outer wall. And around and below that the high water sloshes, blue with reflected sky on its surface, black with shadow and mud and who knows what else beneath.

A gust blows up and over us, almost like the cave is exhaling. Its breath is damp. Cold as buried stones.

I feel the same trembling I've felt whenever I've come here, close to the cave, and during the few times I've stepped inside it. The sensation of everything around me being not just alive, but watchful. Of life after life after life layered in one place. Of the past, all its hidden stories, pulsing against my skin.

If Max feels it too, it's not slowing him down. He's climbing onto another broken rock.

"Careful," I say.

But Max has his hands on the ground now and is creeping even lower. "If I get down here, I think I can see inside," he calls up to me.

He puts one shoe down on the next rock shelf.

I watch the shoe slip. The rock is wet, slimy with rotting leaves and river muck. Max tilts, grabbing the rock with both hands as his foot slides down into the water, almost dragging the rest of his body with it.

I grasp his arm and wrench him upward.

Max gets both feet under him again, the dry one and the soaking wet. He stares at me, breathing hard. I stare back. Something moves between us, like an electric shock: something sharper and stronger than the tremble that's still shaking under my feet.

I let go of his arm.

He probably would have been fine. Even if he'd fallen. There's no undertow here in the little bay; the water's not too deep. But there are unexpected spots where it does plunge down. There are sharp rocks hidden under the surface.

Max manages a grin. "Okay. So *that* was the water I was supposed to look out for."

I shake my head and give a tiny smile back. "Come on," I say, turning around. "And watch your step this time."

Max follows obediently. I can hear his left foot making intermittent soft squishes inside its sodden shoe.

We move back along the ridge, through the trees that lean outward from the bluff like spokes in an open paper fan. The ground levels. The ridge widens. Behind me, I hear Max stop.

"Whoa," he says.

I turn around.

He's bending low, examining something on the ground.

I brush through the long grass to stand beside him.

He's found a bone. A large one. Long and straight and bare and grayish, as though it has been pulled from a heap of ashes.

Because, I realize, it probably has.

People camp around here. They cook over open fires. Those are the most comfortable explanations.

But what I did with Jake and Colton and Kyle and Bailey the other night is another. Generations of Black Point kids gathering around fires in the woods, passing down traditions they barely understand. It's easy to imagine some earlier group neglecting to clean up afterward, forgetting to rake the seared earth smooth and scatter it with leaves. Forgetting to check the cinders for what hasn't burned.

Max cranes forward. He picks up the bone by one end, carefully, and looks from it to me.

I keep my face blank.

"Do you think it's human?" he asks.

I snort softly. Minneapolis. Maybe he's never even seen an animal bone up close.

"Definitely not. Probably a deer leg. Or some farm animal," I add carefully. "Another animal might have dragged it here."

"And then . . . barbecued it?" Max turns the blackened bone around.

It does look a bit like a human femur. Just a little bit.

But it isn't.

"More likely a coyote took it from someone's burn pile." I reach for the bone. Max lets me take it. "There are all kinds of bones out here, all around us," I say. "It's a healthy forest. Things live and die in it. Grandpa and I found a black bear skull once. Teeth and everything."

Max nods, although the thought of bones all around us doesn't seem to please him much.

I raise the bone over my shoulder. Then I throw it, hard and fast, through the trees, toward the water. It strikes with a small splash and goes under.

"Oh, damn," says Max. "We should have brought that to Maeve's store. She'd have made it into a wind chime or something."

I laugh, brushing away the scratch of wrongness that's prickling my skin. The thoughts of the other night. The reminder that Max is an outsider. That none of this will last.

"Come on," I tell him, turning away.

As we wind back through the long grass, my phone buzzes in my pocket.

I pull it out.

A message. From Jake Meier.

Happy birthday!

My stomach twists. I shove the phone back into my pocket.

I leap over a small stream, heading back toward the rise where we left the bag of gas station snacks. From right behind me, Max's foot gives another loud squish as it lands.

"Walking around in that soaked shoe can't be comfortable," I say. "Sorry about that."

He waves one hand. "It's my own fault. And seeing this place totally makes up for it anyway."

This makes me smile. But I tuck my chin low, so he won't see.

Maybe this can't last. Not for real. But its newness, its temporariness, is part of what makes it special. It's the ice cream you have to eat before it melts away.

"Hey," I ask over my shoulder. "Want to go somewhere else you haven't been before?"

April 11, 1986

Hey Matt,

So, I haven't gotten anything from you yet. It's only been a couple days since I asked for the money, I know, but I'm hoping you've at least gotten some of my letters by now. The Hanssons should have sent the first ones off about a week ago. Anyway, whenever you get this, would you send some cash before you forget? Because you do that sometimes. Like with Alicia's last birthday. (SEE, ALICIA? ONE OF US STILL REMEMBERS!)

Jeanne paid me a hundred bucks in cash yesterday, which seems decent when room and board and everything are thrown in. But then I went over to Swede's Garage and talked to Les, this skinny guy who's a hotel regular, and asked him how quick he could get the truck running again. He put on one of those faces, the kind you don't ever want to see on a mechanic or a dentist, and a hundred bucks started to seem pretty small pretty quick.

He said the labor might be seventy bucks or so, but there was more wrong with the truck than they'd thought at first, and a couple things had to be replaced, and he'd had to order parts that might not come in for a while. Maybe a week or more.

I said, "A WEEK?" He looked at me all weird

and asked, "You in a hurry to get out of here or something?"

And I said, no, not at all, because I don't want to seem suspicious. I said I just needed to get moving pretty soon, and Les said something about Jeanne being such a great lady, and how a job at the hotel must be the best gig in town. And then I started to feel kind of stupid again, running away from someplace where I'm safe and fed and two nice ladies wash my socks for me.

Maybe I AM stupid. (I know what you're thinking, Matt. That there's no maybe about it.) I mean, what if I just decided to stay here for a while? Be Neil Schmidt, work at this place, never see the Meyer's Warehouse guys or dad again? Black Point might even start to feel like home.

I can almost picture it. But not quite.

Anyway, I told Les if he could get started now, like, if I prepaid for the parts so he knew I'd be good for it all, that would be great. So I gave him my hundred bucks.

It wasn't quite happy hour yet when I got back to the hotel. Maeve was behind the bar. I asked if she needed me to do anything, but she waved me off, so I headed up to my room. My door was locked when I turned the key. I heard the lock click and everything. And it seemed like that click was opening a door in my own head, showing me that all the ghost stuff could have been in my head too. I mean, maybe Jeanne had finished a cigarette while changing the sheets in my room or something. Maybe I'd forgotten to lock the door once or twice. And if I had, would I have any real reason to run away from this place, like I already ran away from home?

Probably not.

See? I'm not so stupid that I can't answer my own simple questions.

So I was about to step through the door when I saw something moving around a corner just over my shoulder.

And I swear to god, Matt. It was someone in a long white dress.

I turned around.

There was nobody in the hall. But down at the end, just past the restroom, I saw the edge of something white sliding over the floor.

I swear, Matt. Swear to god.

So I followed it.

I had to, or I'd have thought I was going crazy. Like you probably already do.

Past the restroom, at the end of the hall, there's

this little doorway I'd never noticed before. The door was wide open. On the other side was a set of wooden plank stairs leading upward. There was no place else that white dress could have gone.

I climbed the steps.

Don't think I was being super brave or anything. It was broad daylight, and I knew other people weren't far away. I just had to see what was up there.

The steps went up to the fourth floor. The attic. One big room with little windows and lots of junk. There was nobody in it. Just stacks of boxes and heaps of old crap and some racks of clothes. So of course I started to think I WAS crazy after all, even though this cold feeling kept running all over me.

Anyway, I looked around a little, making sure no one was hiding anywhere. I didn't see anyone, and I didn't hear anyone. The piles of crap turned out to be old hotel junk mostly, lamps with dented shades, stacks of bedspreads, stuff like that. The boxes were full of all kinds of other stuff, I suppose things that guests have lost over the years. Weird old shoes. Hats with flowers on them. A ton of books. I wasn't really looking through anything, just sort of skimming it all, when my eyes hit on a bird-watching book.

Nope, I haven't gotten into birds all the sudden. But my mind went straight to the drowned man. The townies said he was a bird-watcher.

I mean, what if that book was his? What if some of the other old stuff up there was his? Would that make the whole story true? I moved toward the bird-watching book so fast that I almost tripped over another open box. I looked down. This box was full of clothes, jewelry, a purse, a bunch of tubes of lipstick.

LIPSTICK, Matt. Like Lipstick Lady.

Okay. So, I was standing by this open box, and my eyes caught something white just ahead of me. It wasn't moving now. It was just hanging there on one of the racks. But it was long and made of fabric and it was exactly the same shade of white I'd seen in the hallway a minute before. And yes, white can have different shades. Or hues. Or tints. Or whatever. I don't know, I didn't pay that much attention in art class.

Crap. My thoughts keep running away from me. I guess they don't want to focus on this anymore.

I know what you're thinking. JUST STOP RAMBLING AND WRITE IT, NEIL.

Okay. Well.

I went closer to the clothing rack. Toward the white thing.

And Matt.

It was an old wedding dress.

I looked around the attic again, making sure, I mean SURE, that I was alone up there.

But then I heard footsteps. I swear my heart stopped, Matt. A second later, Jeanne's curly gray head came up over the top of the staircase. She had a crate full of soap dishes in her hands. She didn't look shocked to see me there. I mean, not as shocked as I must have looked, standing there, gaping back at her like a doofus. But her eyebrows went up, and then they went way down, and she looked all around the room before looking back at me again.

"Neil? What are you doing up here?" she asked.

She looked kind of suspicious. Not ANGRY suspicious. But I saw her eyes go to the boxes of stuff again, and I realized she must have thought I was stealing something. That, or I was snooping, poking around in someone else's things. Which I guess I was.

I said something about coming up to make sure no one had left a window open, because it looked like it was going to rain again. Pretty lame, but it's not like I could tell her I'd just seen a ghost.

Maeve I might have told. But not Jeanne. She's one of those no-nonsense people who's not freaked out by anything. I've seen her crush a spider with her bare hand. A BIG spider.

So Jeanne stared at me for a second. Then she explained that they keep guest room storage up in the attic, all the old supplies and bedding and things that guests have left behind. She said she supposed they could just throw that stuff out, but she hates to do that in case a guest ever comes back for something, and she's got plenty of space to keep it all up here anyway. And then she said—here's the kicker, Matt—she said I could take anything I wanted or needed from the fourth floor. Books, clothes, whatever. All I had to do was ask.

It doesn't take a whole lot to make me feel like scum. I've done some scummy things. But now I KNEW I was scum. A whole bucket of scum.

I said no thanks, but that it was really nice of her, and then I scuttled back down to my room before my face could get any redder.

Here's the next weird thing, though. When I passed her, I swear for a second Jeanne gave me a different kind of look. Not a nice one. And I swear again, after she looked at me, she looked over at the boxes where I'd been standing, and then straight at the hanging wedding dress.

So either I'm an ungrateful snooping nutjob, or this place is actually haunted, and nobody and nothing in it wants me here.

Either way I guess it's time to leave. No more changing my mind.

If you could send me that cash, Matt, even a little, so I can get the truck running and head out, that would be great. Neil SCHMIDT, remember.

Oh—and like you must have noticed, I'm wrapping this letter in an extra sheet of paper before I seal it up. I always put these letters in the pile to be mailed along with all the other hotel stuff, and I'm not saying I don't trust the Hanssons, but just in case they can see their names or anything right through the envelope, I should be careful.

Maybe that's crazy. Just another mark in the ungrateful nutjob column, right?

Right.

—Neil

8

I SHOULD HAVE SENSED SOMETHING.

I should have felt it as Max and I walked up to my old brick house at the top of Fourth Street. I should have noticed the familiar cars parked not so inconspicuously around the corner, all the lights on, the flicker of motion behind the lace curtains. But I didn't.

I was already thinking about what Mom and Grandpa would do, about how they would feel that I'd brought a stranger home for my birthday dinner. At the same time, I was listening to Max, who was asking if I was sure my family wouldn't mind him just showing up, and I was telling him that it would be totally fine, that the three of us would need help eating a whole cake anyway, all while trying to ignore the fizz of excitement and nervousness sloshing inside my stomach.

So when I open the kitchen door and a wall of voices screams "*SURPRISE!!*" it works.

I jump backward, colliding with Max. My heel drops over the edge of the top step. His arm reaches up to catch me. I feel it, warm and solid against my shoulder blades, before I stiffen up and he lets go.

The kitchen is full of people.

Mom and Grandpa, of course. The Oldies: Les, Duane, Chuck. Cara and Bailey. And because the Oldies love pulling strings, there are Jake, Colton, and Kyle. They're all beaming at me, faces locked in broad smiles. Then their eyes flick to the boy behind me. I see every single expression change, one after another, like a row of falling dominoes. There's confusion. Surprise. Annoyance, or something harsher, from Les and Chuck. Everything has gone from comfortable and right to uncomfortable and wrong in the time it takes to blink.

"Oh my gosh." I force a laugh. "You literally knocked me over."

Mom is still smiling, but it's a more fragile smile now, like the china that only gets brought out for dinner with company. Cara and Bailey take small steps forward, not sure what to do next.

I'm not sure either. It was already a leap, showing up with Max. It would have been enough with just Mom and Grandpa here. But throw in a whole surprise party and everything feels amplified, distorted, out of proportion.

"I can't believe you all planned this," I say, moving toward my friends.

"It wasn't hard to keep it a secret," says Cara, giving me a quick, stiff squeeze. "I haven't even *seen* you in weeks."

"I know. I've just been so busy, with the museum—"

"Sure," she cuts in. "Me too. I've got all those college visits, and I'm working crazy hours at the fruit stand. But I get all the free strawberries and free bee stings I could want, so . . ." She doesn't finish.

Bailey's hug is longer, but it's stiffer than normal too. "I haven't seen you in forever either!" she says loudly.

I see what's happening here. We're going to pretend the other night in the woods never happened. We're going to lie to everyone, even ourselves.

Bailey's eyes flick to the stranger standing behind me.

"Happy birthday, old lady," she adds, backing away again.

Jake, Colton, and Kyle don't move any closer. The three of them are watching Max like this is a school assembly and he's our vice principal. There's the same tightly lidded hostility in their eyes.

Jake manages a quick wave in my direction. "Happy birthday," he murmurs.

I turn to Grandpa, whose sharp eyes are the only ones fixed fully on me.

"Grandpa, you've already met m—" I almost say "my." My what? My friend? "Max." Thank god his name starts with the same *M* sound. "You've kind of met him, anyway. This is Max Nazarian. His aunt bought the hotel. He's helping her out."

"Of course." Mom hurries over before Grandpa can answer.

She puts on her front desk voice. "Hello. I'm Beth Sorenson. Nice to meet you. And welcome."

Max shakes her hand. "Thanks." His face wears the same unreadable mask as when I first met him.

I turn back to Grandpa and the Oldies. "And these are the guys from the museum," I tell Max. "Les, and Duane, and Chuck."

The Oldies shake Max's hand with that brief but extra-firm shake old guys do. Over my shoulder, I hear Bailey whispering something to Cara, but I can't pick up the words.

"Good to meet you," Grandpa says, shaking Max's hand last. He sounds polite and pleasant, like with tourists at the museum. Not quite himself.

"Well," says Max, stepping backward. "I should go. You all have special plans."

"No, no," says my mom, with perfect knee-jerk courtesy. "Stay. We have too much food as it is. Unless you have somewhere else you need to be . . ."

The line is mildly prying, asking about his life without actually asking, and at the same time implying that he can't have any other plans. Not in this town.

"Nope," says Max. "Nothing."

"Good, good." Mom repeats herself when she's stalling. "Then you'll join us for supper."

There's a silent beat.

Grandpa speaks up, and I don't know if I've ever been more grateful.

"So," he says to Max, "what do you think of Black Point?"

"It's nice," Max answers. "Peaceful. Lucia just showed me this really beautiful spot down by the river."

The Oldies' eyes all flash to me. I expect teasing. But there's only coldness. Unfamiliar coldness.

"She did, huh," says Chuck.

And it's not a question.

Not for Max, anyway.

"What can I get everyone to drink?" Mom cuts in. "Les? Duane?"

Cara's hand closes around my arm. "Hey," she whispers, close to my ear. "What's going on?" The Oldies are occupied now, so I turn to face her wide eyes and smirking mouth. "Are you, like, *with* that guy?"

"We were just hanging out," I murmur back.

Cara's eyebrows rise. "Hanging out?"

"I was showing him around town. That's all."

Behind me, the Oldies have gone quiet again. The three younger guys have formed a separate silent knot on the far side of the room. A weight settles over the kitchen like humid air.

"Well!" Mom's voice breaks through, unnaturally loud. "Lucia, why don't you lead the way to the table? Everyone else, take a seat. Help yourselves!"

Max sits down in the chair to my left.

It would be wrong to expect him to sit anywhere else. I invited him; I'm clearly the only person who wants him here. But having him beside me feels wrong too. Like physical proof of something that might not even be real.

Grandpa and the Oldies spend the dinner working through muted versions of their usual numbers: who bought what, who sold it, who's sick and how bad. Bailey and Cara talk about their summer jobs and weekend plans. Jake, Kyle, and Colton barely talk at all, except for one long trip into the world of high school wrestling, led by Coach Les. My mom keeps interrupting all the other conversations to make sure everyone has gotten seconds on the sandwiches and chips and coleslaw.

Suddenly, in a lull, Les turns to Max. "Where did you say you were from?" he asks.

It's as though a spotlight has switched on just above Max's chair. Everyone turns to look.

"Minneapolis," Max answers.

Although the Oldies already know this. I *told* them this. I know they haven't forgotten.

"Northeast Minneapolis," Max adds, when Les keeps staring.

"What about your family?" Les asks. "Where are they from?"

I know what Les is really asking.

Max knows too. I see it in the tiny change in the edges of his mouth. I wonder how often he's been asked this question. I wonder how often he's been asked since he got to Black Point.

"My mom was born in Chicago," he says. "My dad grew up mostly in California. My family came from Armenia, originally."

"So you're Armenian?" Bailey says. "Like the Kardashians?"

Which is both the worst and best thing she could have said.

"Ohhhh . . ." says Cara.

Chuck blinks. "Like who?"

But everyone else has the look of vague recognition on their faces. Familiar ground.

"Yeah," says Max, deadpan. "We're *just* like the Kardashians."

Bailey giggles.

"Let's get to the main event, shall we?" Mom shoves back her chair and bustles across the kitchen to a cake on a cardboard tray.

She carries it to the table. *Happy birthday, Lucia!* shouts the blue frosting, surrounded by the massive pink and red icing roses that are the Lindholms' Bakery signature.

Mom lights the candles. She starts the song, and everyone around the table joins in. I can hear Max's voice beside me, low and soft, but in tune.

That's when my cheeks start to burn.

I've hauled this boy all over my town. Into my house. Into the middle of my own surprise birthday party. All on the very first whole day we spent together. *First*, I catch myself thinking, as though there could be another after this.

It's all wrong. It's all so much more wrong than I imagined it would be. I can't look at the Oldies. I can't even look at my Grandpa. Not without seeing something I don't want to see.

"Happy birth-day, dear Loo-see-ya . . . Happy birthday to you!"

I blow out the candles as fast as I can. I wish I could bury my face in the mounds of frosting roses.

We eat cake. Presents come next. The Oldies have pooled their money to get me a Black Point High School class ring, which I didn't want, but it's generous anyway. Jake and Colton and Kyle have chipped in on a gift card for the gas station, because of course they did. Bailey and Cara give me gag gifts: the DVD of a terrible old horror movie that gave us nightmares for months when we were eleven, an entire grocery sack full of Swedish Fish.

Mom's gift to me is an illustrated book of Scandinavian folk-tales. As I flip open the cover, several computer-printed pages slip out from inside. Pages of information on college mythology and folklore programs. History programs. Anthropology programs. I see UW–Madison. St. Olaf. Even Northwestern, all the way down in Chicago.

I look at Mom over the sheaf of papers.

"I did a little research for you," she says. "It's a librarian thing. I couldn't help myself. I just thought you might be interested."

As if I don't know how Google works. As if I don't know what's really going on here.

I can't even force myself to say thank you.

The Oldies look like they've turned to stone. Grandpa's eyes are fixed on the wall somewhere to the left of all of us. Somehow, impossibly, this night has gotten even worse.

"Hey," says Cara, breaking through the crust of silence. "You've got one more box to open."

I reach for the small square package.

Inside is a pendant on a thin silver chain. I tug it out so it catches the light.

"Bergquist made it," Grandpa says, his voice a bit gruff. "It's modeled after a key found in Skåne, Sweden, probably dating from the ninth century. But it actually opens the museum doors."

I know—and Grandpa knows I know—that Viking women wore keys like jewelry, to show ownership of a place and its contents. I know what it means that he's given this to me.

My mother knows too. She sits across the table, eyes moving from Grandpa to me. Her body is suddenly so tense I can almost hear it vibrating.

I raise my chin. "I love it," I tell Grandpa, slipping the chain over my head. "Thank you, Grandpa."

He meets my eyes and smiles. His real smile. Finally.

Mom jumps up and starts gathering the wrapping paper, crumpling it loudly in both hands. A clear sign that the party is over.

It's only midevening, but the Oldies start the shuffle toward the door. It usually takes them at least twenty minutes to make their exit, remembering one more story, one more fact, but tonight, the layers of wrongness seem to push them out.

"I'd better see you three burning off that cake in the weight room this week!" Les calls back to the younger guys as he goes.

Jake and Colton and Kyle head toward the door next. Jake keeps shooting looks back at Max, like he's waiting for him to leave first, but Max doesn't seem to notice—or refuses to show it if he has.

Jake nudges my arm on his way past. "See you soon, Lucia," he says loudly.

Of course we'll see each other soon. This is too small a place to avoid anyone, even if you try. But Jake has made it sound like we have plans. And I'm sure that's just what he meant to do.

"Bye," I answer.

Finally, the three guys head out the door, and I swear I catch a wisp of bonfire smoke in their wake.

Cara and Bailey trail after. Once, they would have stayed; we would have huddled up in my room, talking, laughing, watching videos. But that's not going to happen now, and we all know it. Not with what's coming next. Not with what's already here.

When I close the screen door behind them and step back into the kitchen, Mom and Grandpa are busy clearing up, bustling around, making more noise than two people need to. And Max stands like an island in the middle of the kitchen floor.

He steps toward me. "I should get going too."

I nod. "Sorry about . . . all of this. I honestly had no idea."

"I know." He flashes a short smile. "Thank you, Mrs. Sorenson. And Mr. Sorenson."

"You're very welcome." Mom glances up from the sink with another front desk smile. "Have a good night, now."

Grandpa doesn't say anything.

For a second, Max and I waver in the doorway. I don't know what I'm expecting. What could possibly make this strangeness right. I try and try, but I can't even imagine an answer.

Max meets my eyes. He gives me another smile. A small, secret one. "Good night," he says.

Then he steps out the screen door.

I shut it behind him. This time I close the inner door too.

Mom is piling dishes in the sink. I'm still so angry at her, for the judgment hidden inside her present, that my jaw clenches as I walk past. Grandpa is clearing the table. I grab a wadded paper napkin before he can reach for it.

"Hey, it's your birthday," says Grandpa. "You're supposed to lounge and be lazy."

"Hey, it's my birthday. I'll do what I want."

We work quietly for a moment. I bend over the table to grab a fork, and the key on its silver chain swings.

"He'll go back to Minneapolis pretty soon, I suppose," says Grandpa.

He doesn't need to use a name. Maybe he doesn't want to.

"I guess. By the end of summer, anyway," I answer. "But maybe he'll come back sometimes, to help. I mean, as long as his aunt owns the hotel."

Grandpa nods once, heading toward the garage with the armful of trash. "And who knows how long that'll last."

Of course a bistro and cidery won't last.

It doesn't belong here.

And I do. I'm needed. I'm the key that fits the lock. Everything else—old friends, new friends, people and their businesses and their ideas—can come and go. I'm part of something that will last.

Something sacred.

After giving me a kiss on the head, Grandpa heads toward his room at the end of the downstairs wing. Mom and I are left alone in the kitchen.

Before I can stalk away, she says, "So, did you like your party?"

I stop near the table. "It was nice. Except for the college guilt thing."

"Luce . . ." Mom sighs. She dips a platter into the bubbly sink. "You need to give it some more thought. That's all." She rinses the suds away. "You've got so many options. More than you'll ever have again."

Now it's my turn to sigh.

I'm tired of this speech. I've already made my choice. I don't need others.

Mom lifts a soapy plate. "This town . . . it might not be the best place for you, Lucia. Not forever. There aren't a lot of opportunities here. With time, there will be less and less. I just—I just think you should see what else is out there, while you still have the chance."

"*You* stayed here." I cross to the sink and lean on the counter beside her. "You went to college half an hour away, and then you moved straight back. Even though Dad never wanted to be here at all."

"You know why I did that," Mom answers in her patient librarian voice. "I had to be here for my parents. My mother was in cancer treatment. My dad had heart issues. I wanted to help them, and I wanted to raise you close to them. And I got a good job right here at the library—"

"You're basically describing my exact situation," I break in. "I want to be here for my family. And for the town. And I've already got my dream job waiting for me."

"Okay. You're right," my mom concedes. "I came back. But that doesn't mean it's the best way. The only way. It doesn't mean it's the best thing for *you*." She rinses her hands and turns to face me. Her voice is low, like she's afraid someone will overhear. "I know you love this place. But maybe you're up too close to see its flaws. Because this isn't a healthy town, Lucia. It won't be here forever."

"It won't be if everyone who cares about it leaves it."

"Listen. Luce." Mom wraps one warm hand around my wrist. "There were things I didn't realize about this town when I was your age. Even though I'd grown up here. I didn't know what it would be like to stay here for good. To run out of chances to do anything else." She looks hard into my eyes. Hers are panicky and sad. They make me want to pull away. "I want you to have *every* chance."

"What if that's not what *I* want?" I say.

Then I shove away from the counter and head upstairs, wishing I could leave the burrowing wrongness in my chest behind me too.

April 13, 1986

Hey Matt,

Still haven't gotten any answers from you. I mean, I know you're busy, and I know it must be tough to keep all of this hidden from dad, but I'm just saying.

Alicia IS passing these letters on to you, right? You guys didn't break up or anything? I know you might've done something dumb enough to get yourself dumped, but Alicia's so nice I bet she'd still pass my letters along. (YOU'RE A QUEEN, ALICIA.) So I'm hoping you're getting these letters and just haven't had the chance to write back. But if you could do that soon, Matt, it'd be good. Otherwise I might have to do something illegal to get some extra cash.

Just kidding.

Of course, if everybody believes you already DID something illegal, you might as well do something illegal that would actually pay off, right?

Ha ha.

Anyway. You want to hear something crazy?

Remember what I wrote before, about finding the cigarette butt in my locked room? Yesterday night, after dinner, when the bar closed and every-

body went home or up to their rooms, I headed up to mine too. My door was shut and locked, like I'd left it. I always triple-check it now. And then sometimes I check it again.

I'm going to leave here with no money and a bunch of weird habits, Matt.

Anyway, the door was locked. I opened it with my key and locked it again behind me. I turned on the light and looked around. All my stuff was where it belonged. But the glass ashtray was out in the middle of the bedside table again. And there was a cigarette in it. The same kind I found in the ashtray before. All white, even the filter part. Except for a little bit of pink lipstick on the end.

It was a Kent. I checked.

Jeanne smokes Marlboros. I know for sure, because she sent me down to the gas station to pick up a carton once.

And I didn't spot it until I was close, but next to the ashtray was a little gold lighter engraved with the letter C. Want to know what an idiot I am? My first thought was "Lipstick Lady doesn't start with a C."

I'm serious.

But obviously that ghost, the Lipstick Lady who the townies were talking about—she had a name once. Something like Carol or Cheryl. Like that private investigator had said to Jeanne the other day. Like the missing woman.

I want you to imagine me looking really brave and tough during this next part, okay? Because I can hardly believe I did it at all.

I snuck back up to the attic.

There are no lights up there. This was something I hadn't noticed before, and it was really crappy to notice it now, in the pitch dark, with god knows how many ghosts floating around. I used the gold lighter to see my way across the room, and then I spotted an old oil lamp in one of the heaps of junk, because of course there's an old oil lamp up there. So I lit the lamp and found my way back to the box I'd noticed before. The one with the lipstick and clothes and stuff in it. I dug through it as fast as I could.

I checked the purse first, but there was no wallet or ID or anything. Way down at the bottom, though, I found a tangled little wad of necklaces. One chain had a gold charm engraved with another letter C.

My heart started thumping like a whole marching band.

Next to the purse was an old Life *magazine.*

March 1965 issue. Twenty years ago, just like that investigator had said.

And sort of crushed under the purse was a half-empty pack of cigarettes. I pulled them out and held them up to the light.

Kents. Freaking Kents, Matt. Swear to god.

I don't remember how I got back down to my room. I think I left the lighter in the box along with all the other stuff, and I know I brought the oil lamp down with me, because the damn thing is sitting on my desk right now and I'll have to sneak it back upstairs again.

I didn't sleep for the rest of the night. I just thought about everything and gave myself a giant headache, and all I came away with was a bunch of questions. Like C has to be the Carol or Cheryl or whoever that went missing around here twenty-some years ago, right? And if she is, then is she—or her ghost or whatever the hell you become when you die—trying to be found?

Hey, Matt. You remember when we went to see Alicia in that play a year ago? You'd better say yes. (YOU WERE GREAT IN THE PLAY, ALICIA!) *It was called* Arsenic and Lace *or something. Remember, it was about two sweet old ladies who ran this little inn where they kept killing people and burying them in the basement? Okay. So, it's totally crazy of me to think that something like that might be going on here, right? I mean, especially when Jeanne and Maeve have been so nice to me and all I've got for proof is some townie gossip and some weird ghost clues. So I shouldn't even think about that. Right? But if C is the missing person, and if Jeanne put her stuff up there in the attic in the first place and kept it all this time, then when that investigator stopped by the hotel,* WHY THE HELL DID JEANNE LIE?

My best guess is that somebody is messing with me. Leaving the cigarettes and footprints and other clues around. Unlocking my door. Freaking me out.

But why would they want to?

Beats the heck out of me.

Feel free to chime in with any theories, Matt. Send them along with that money.

—Neil

9

The morning after my birthday party, half an hour before opening time, I reach the museum's front doors. The sky above is heavy gray, the kind that could belong to morning or evening, and the air feels thick with oncoming rain. The last thing we need.

The doors are locked, just as they should be preopening. Instead of the old key I kept on a loop in my pocket, I take the silver key on its chain around my neck and fit it into the front door for the first time. It turns with a click, and I step inside, into the familiar museum smells of old wood and lemon polish and faint, smoky cologne.

Grandpa is nowhere to be seen on the main floor. He'd left the house before I even got downstairs for breakfast this morning. But Les and Duane are at the front desk, sorting papers, getting ready for the day. They both look up at me.

"Hey, it's the birthday girl," says Les loudly. "Feeling a year older and a year wiser?"

"A little older," I tell them. "No wiser."

"Well, good," says Duane. "We don't want you getting too smart for us."

There's a beat.

We're all thinking about last night. About me dragging a strange boy into the middle of my surprise party. At least I'm wise enough not to do that again.

"I wish I'd known you were all planning something special," I begin, awkwardly. "I mean, I guess that would've ruined the surprise, but then I wouldn't–"

I'm cut off by a sound from downstairs.

Grandpa.

He's shouting something. I can't tell if it's *Hey* or *Here* or if it's a name. But it's a shout.

I've never heard him shout this loudly or sharply before, not even when he was teaching me to drive on winter roads and I skidded straight off an icy curve on County J and into an eight-foot snowbank.

Fear spikes through me, sharp and clear as an icicle.

I think I fly down the staircase. I don't remember my shoes touching a single step, or my hand grasping the rail. I'm hurtling downward, and then I land on the hardwood floor, heart drumming, lungs frozen.

Grandpa is standing at one side of the downstairs room.

Standing.

Thank god.

At first, that's all I can see: that he's upright. When I get closer—which takes two seconds and eight hundred years—I can tell that he's not wounded. He's breathing. He's standing. His face isn't collapsed in pain.

Relief pounds through me. It's not his heart. This isn't the moment. He's all right. He's all right.

But he isn't.

He's staring at one of the windows near the basement's emergency door. I turn to stare too. The glass in the window is broken. Shards spatter the gold wood floorboards below. I don't see a rock, or a brick, or anything else someone could have thrown through the jagged hole, if things like that ever happened around here. But someone could have broken the glass and opened the emergency door by reaching through.

And that must be what they did. Because now that I can look anywhere else, I notice the other broken things. The cracked case of replica seaxes. The rack that used to display some old Swedish farming tools hanging bare and crooked on its wall. The glass box for the possessions of the town founders—Jan Lundberg's pocketknife, Hans Hansson's firesteel, Lars Angstrom's compass, Varg Sorenson's long knife—is smashed to glitter. The contents are gone.

Everything inside my body, everything that usually holds me up, disappears too. I grab the edge of a display case with one hand. Broken glass scrapes my palm.

"Oh my god," I hear myself say.

Duane and Les thud down the stairs behind me. Their footsteps halt as they freeze, taking in the scene.

"What the hell happened here?" Les asks.

Grandpa turns toward us. His face is tired. Not angry or sad or anything else. Just tired. "Somebody broke in."

"And stole something?" says Les.

"Looks like," Grandpa answers.

"What's missing?" Duane takes a couple steps forward. I can see the former cop in him: the way his stance hardens, the set of his face.

"A few things," says Grandpa softly. He looks at the empty pedestal where the founders' things should be. "A few things."

The next hours are a blur. Duane calls the police; Karl Anderson and Don Ekblad are up the hill in about two minutes. While they and Duane and Grandpa examine the lower floor and check security camera footage, Les phones Chuck, who rushes over, and then Auer's Glass and the hardware store. I make a sign reading "Closed Today—Sorry for the Inconvenience" to hang out front and post the same message online, because I'm the only one who knows how. Finally, once the police and the Oldies trudge upstairs and give me the all clear, I head down with the big broom and dustpan.

There's no way I'm letting Grandpa do this job.

The shattered glass shimmers as I scrape it into the trash can. Rain is just beginning to fall. Rising winds push the droplets through the broken window, spattering my arms and face. Taunting me. But all I feel is numb. Hollowed. Like the loss has invaded everything.

By the time I get back upstairs, Karl and Don are gone. Grandpa and Les and Duane and Chuck are gathered at the front desk, their voices tighter and lower than usual, watching clips of security footage again and again.

I crane around Chuck's bony shoulder. The images on the computer screen are grainy, but I can make out two guys, youngish, unfamiliar, dressed in sweatshirts with deep hoods.

"See, I swear that one says Timberwolves," says Les, pointing at one of the shirts.

"Probably not from around here," adds Duane.

"Exactly how much did they take? Besides the stuff in the founders' case?" I ask. Saying the words aloud makes my stomach roil. "Do we have a list?"

"Three seaxes–replicas. Five antique farming tools. And the founders' things, like you said." Grandpa's voice rasps a little at the end, like just saying the words is painful. "Items that are valuable to us, but that aren't all that valuable to anyone else."

"More likely a couple of stupid kids than experienced thieves." Duane folds his arms over his broad chest. "They didn't try to get into the register. They're not doing this for profit."

Grandpa nods. "They didn't even come upstairs."

"Thank goodness," says Les.

Maybe I should feel thankful too. But luck and ignorance don't seem like much to be grateful for.

"Hey," I say, taking another look at Grandpa. "You should sit down."

I hook one of the nearby folding chairs with my foot and drag it close to us. For once, Grandpa doesn't argue. He just sinks down onto the seat.

Not a good sign.

Something inside my chest starts to thrum.

"Wonder if they drove down from the Cities," says Chuck.

Duane tips his head. "Or maybe they're new to the area."

I feel the Oldies' eyes flick to me.

Les and Duane have known me since the day I was born. I'm not going to pretend I don't understand them now.

"You mean Max?" I ask.

The Oldies keep quiet.

"Let me see the video again," I say.

Duane clicks a button. I lean close to the screen.

One of the guys is large, round faced, pale. Definitely not Max. The other is a little shorter. Most of his face is hidden inside his hood. But he doesn't move the way Max moves. He's high shouldered and quick, and when he turns, there's no choppy dark hair across his forehead as far as I can make out.

But I could be wrong. I could be misremembering. I could

have put too much trust in someone I don't actually know at all.

Duane shrugs. "Doesn't really look like him," he says. "But he's been in this place more than once already. Hung around. Maybe he's got friends who'd do something dumb."

My thoughts streak to our talk out at the Bend. About his parents wanting to separate him from the friends who'd gotten him into trouble. *Disturbing the peace. A tiny bit of breaking and entering.*

Jesus. I'm an idiot.

The thing in my chest thrums harder.

"Play it one more time?" I ask Duane.

I don't want to see it. But the broken pieces are starting to form a picture, one that tells me this is all my fault.

I'm still staring at the video when a buzz snaps through the air.

It's a cell phone. All of our cell phones. Grandpa, Les, Duane, and Chuck fumble for theirs, frowning down at the screens. I pull mine from my pocket.

Severe thunderstorm warning. Potential flooding. Of course. The whole county, and the ones north of us too. More water sluicing downstream. More ground worn away. And I feel like I'm standing knee-deep in the muddy river right now, trying to push it back with both hands.

"Damn it," I hear Les mutter.

The Oldies have moved away from me. Even Grandpa has gotten up from the folding chair and stepped out from behind the front desk. They're huddled a few steps off, still holding their phones, although they're not looking at the screens anymore. Just at one another.

"I knew it," mutters Les. "I *knew* it. I said so."

Duane clears his throat.

"Just . . . wait," says Grandpa's deep voice.

They all glance over at me.

There's silence. Except for the rumble and shush of the thickening rain.

"Everything okay?" I ask.

"Just fine," says Grandpa, lifting his chin. He gives me a steady smile. "It will be just fine."

Grandpa doesn't lie to me.

But I know, all the way through the very center of myself, that nothing is just fine.

April 15, 1986

Hey Matt,

Still no letter from you. I really need an answer, okay? Any kind of answer. Don't give me one more reason to freak out.

I mean, I'll keep writing to you either way, because there's no one else around here who I can talk to about that missing woman. Not without it getting straight back to Jeanne and Maeve. But I can't stop thinking about it. YOU try to stop thinking about someone when their stuff keeps showing up in your locked bedroom.

So anyway, yesterday morning I headed over to the library.

Yep. I went to a library. Voluntarily. (OKAY. LAUGH YOUR HEAD OFF, ALICIA.*)*

The Black Point library is pretty small, but I figured it would at least have old newspapers and stuff. And it did, along with one microfiche machine. I was going to look through the local papers from 1965, because you'd think in a place this size, some woman disappearing would be front page news for months.

But nope. I cycled through the old weekly issues of the Black Point Banner until my eyes burned, and the most exciting article I found was about somebody's prize bull being struck by lightning. Swear to god, Matt.

Once I finished all the Black Point Banners for 1965 with no luck, I asked the librarian if they had any other newspapers from the same year. He gave me boxes of film for the Milwaukee Journal Sentinel and the La Crosse Tribune, looking kind of annoyed at me the whole time. But maybe he just doesn't like La Crosse. Or Milwaukee.

I started with La Crosse, because I figured there would be less to look through. I was already feeling tired and stupid and my neck was stiff from sitting at that damn machine. But when I thought about giving up, I remembered that ashtray with the cigarette butt lying in it, and the lighter and that little gold charm, and the fact that, until the truck's working, I'm completely stuck here.

So I kept looking.

And Matt.

I found it.

June 1965. An article about a missing woman, last seen stopping for gas north of La Crosse. Her name was Carole Harran. Age 26. From Chicago. Worked as a temp in a secretarial agency. Police were asking the public for info. The article mentioned that there'd been lots of flooding in the area and that maybe she'd made a wrong turn somewhere and gotten stuck. Or swept away. There was a picture of her with the article: curly hair, big smile. And she was wearing a necklace. The picture was really small and kind of smudged looking, but it COULD have been one of the necklaces I saw in that box upstairs.

Even if it wasn't, everything else matched. Everything. Except I know Carole Harran didn't just get swept away. She made it here. To the Black Point Hotel.

I sat there for a while and tried to think.

Okay. Like Jeanne said, hundreds of people come and go from a hotel over the years. But if you lived in a tiny town like this, wouldn't you remember a story about somebody going missing? Especially if they'd been staying in your hotel when they disappeared, and they'd even left their purse and their jewelry behind?

Ready to laugh again? I wrote down the name and dates and everything important in the article, super carefully. And then I walked straight over to the cop shop.

It's kind of funny that Black Point even has a police department. But I guess the people here need someone to call when their bulls get struck by lightning.

Anyway, I went in and talked to the big bald guy at the desk. I told him I had some information about a woman named Carole Harran who'd disappeared around here twenty-one years ago. I explained about where I worked, and about the stuff I'd found in the attic, and I mentioned the private investigator and how Jeanne had told him she couldn't remember. I tried to make it sound like I didn't doubt Jeanne or anything, but like maybe she'd just overlooked or forgotten something. I really want to believe all that myself.

The cop listened, taking notes, keeping pretty quiet. It was hard to tell if he believed me. I suppose he was just doing that thing cops do when they keep a totally calm face no matter what's happening. And I noticed that his face was really familiar. I tried to think where I might have seen him before, but I couldn't remember running into any cops around here. Then I tried picturing him in something other than a uniform, and that did it.

I'd seen him at the hotel. He comes in almost every night, in slacks and a polo shirt. Drinks an Old Style or two and has dinner with some of the other townie guys, like Les the mechanic and Frank the history buff.

So I said, "Hey, you're a regular at the hotel, aren't you?" And he just gave a quick little nod and smile, no questions, no stopping to think or anything. And that's when I realized that he'd recognized ME all along.

I don't know why, Matt. But that made my guts twist.

He looked up from his notes and asked if there was anything else. I said not that I could think of. He closed his little notebook and told me he'd look into it.

That was it.

I had to run to the hotel to make it in time for the lunch hour. Maeve and Jeanne didn't ask me where I'd been. They were just as nice as always, which made me feel even more guilty and nervous. I broke two glasses, my hands shook so bad.

But I had to do it. Right?

At the very least, maybe I'll get Lipstick Lady—I

adding fresh waves to the river, pushing its edges up and over the lowest local roads.

"I heard Old Gooseneck Road is washed out," says Chuck, pouring himself yet another mug of coffee. His hand around the cup looks like knots on an oak tree. "Larry Elmquist said he had to drive four miles out of the way, all the way up over the hills, to get to town this morning."

"Everything down on the frontage is closed," says Duane. "Bunch of basements on Main are flooded too."

"Can't be looking too good in the hotel," says Les.

The hint under the words is sharp and clear.

The hotel. Max. Anything but good.

Before anybody can answer, Lou sweeps up to the table and plunks down five slices of pie, our favorite kind for each of us, even though it's nowhere near lunchtime yet.

"On the house today," she says, waving off our arguments. "Pay me back by helping catch those lowlifes." She strides away again—but not without aiming a quick glance at me.

Duane's eyes coast over me too. Chuck coughs and reaches for the carafe once more.

I wrap my hand hard around my fork.

"So," says Grandpa. "We'd better talk about Black Point Days."

I set my fork down again.

Black Point Days is our big annual summer festival. There's a parade, a pickled herring and meatball supper, a craft fair, a fireworks show down at Riverside Park. We commemorate the town's founding. We eat a lot of baked goods.

"We're all set with the truck for the parade, right?" Grandpa asks Les.

"All set. The float needs some touch-ups, though. We could do it Thursday or Friday."

The museum runs one of the parade's largest floats: a replica longship with a dragon's head on a long curving neck and BLACK POINT spelled out on wooden shields along its sides. We walk the parade route beside the ship, dressed in old Norse clothes and armor, handing out candy and inflatable plastic swords.

"Black Point Days is still happening?" I ask. "Even with the flooding?"

"Water's high on Black Point Days half the time," Les points out.

"That's the risk of having it in June," says Chuck. "Any other month, there'd be some other problem."

I nod. "It just seems funny. Celebrating the founding of the town when our founders' stuff has just been stolen."

Grandpa puts down his coffee cup. "Are we going to let them steal this from us too?"

Nobody answers. Not aloud. But we all sit up straighter.

Duane gives me a nod and a smile. I smile back.

I'm still holding myself straight when we all step out the door of the café an hour or so later. No, we're not going to let a few weeks of wet weather or a couple of idiot outsiders hurt this town. I'm not going to let them take one more thing.

And then, so suddenly that he might have swooped down from the sky, Max is there. On the sidewalk, right in front of me. I nearly walk into him, and I jerk myself backward just in time.

"Hey," he says, smiling. Choppy dark hair fluttering in the wind. "I was just up at the museum, and I saw the closed signs. Is something wrong?"

Is something wrong? I turn the words over in my head like heavy mud on a spade. Does he really not know? Is he pretending? Would I be able to tell either way?

Rock-faced and silent, the Oldies flank me. Gradually, they step away, like they know I'll want this moment alone. They know I'll handle it.

They send ice-hard looks at Max over their shoulders as they go.

Max looks almost amused now. "Whoa," he says, turning back toward me. "What?"

I point past him, up the hill. "Want to go for a walk?"

"Sure." He steps back to let me lead.

The air is hot, steamed by sun and thick with yesterday's rain. It smells like decaying leaves. I head upward, to where Park Street splits north and south, and Max walks after me.

I didn't really want to trek up a steep hill in this heat. But I'm not going to have this conversation on a sidewalk in the middle of town, surrounded by open shops, staring windows, passing cars.

"So, was there something you needed? Or did you just happen to be walking by the museum this morning?" I try to keep my voice neutral. Even though the words *returning to the scene of the crime* shove their way into my brain.

"Oh." Max looks like he's remembered something. He frowns, then shakes the frown away. "I was just going to ask you about something. It's not a big deal. You've obviously got other stuff going on."

I glance over at him. His face is solemn, shielded. Whatever it is, it isn't nothing. "Tell me."

For a second, Max looks almost uncomfortable. And I don't think it's because of the sticky heat. "Okay," he begins. "Yesterday morning, I found a deer's head on the hotel steps. And some other parts." He hesitates, choosing his words like he's stepping out onto the planks of a bridge. "Organs. Blood. Some things I couldn't even identify."

Sourness fills my mouth. "Ugh," I say softly.

"Yeah."

Max doesn't go on.

I can sense that he's holding back. Not giving details. Not making guesses or excuses.

So I make my own. "An animal must have dragged it there. Probably found it dead on the side of the road. That happens sometimes."

Max's eyes don't meet mine. "I don't think so. Because it was, like . . . arranged."

"Arranged?" I repeat.

"The head was in the middle, facing up. Toward the door. The—other things—were set up on each side. Symmetrically." He gives a small shrug. "Like it was something we were supposed to find."

"That's . . ." Flashes and questions and faces slide through my mind, knocking into every sentence I form. Stained hands clasped around a bonfire. The smell of animal blood in the air. Kyle and Jake's laughter. "That's . . . really weird. I'm sorry."

"Maybe it was just animals, like you said. Or a joke or something. Anyway." Max straightens his shoulders. "I spent the morning cleaning it all up before Ani had to see it." He grins, raising both hands. "And I scrubbed my hands for about half an hour afterward, I swear."

I don't smile back.

I need to stay on the path I chose. I need to remember what really matters.

We reach the fork where the road gets even steeper. A pickup truck coasts down the hill past us. It's far too bright for me to get a look at the driver, but I see a silhouette turning to stare at us as the truck streaks by.

"Where are we going?" Max asks mildly.

"The cemetery," I answer.

"You have some burying to do?"

"It's shady," I tell him. "And quiet."

I step off the paved road onto the gravel track that leads through the wrought iron gates. On the arch hang the words *Black Point Cemetery—1870.*

The cemetery stretches along the hillside just above downtown Black Point. The graves in their even rows face the rows of houses below, like the dead are keeping an eye on the places that were once theirs. That are still theirs, in a way.

My whole family is here. From my great-great-great-great-grandpa, town founder Varg Sorenson, all the way to Grandma Kay. The roots of my tree.

I head through the towering pines and cedars and oaks, Max close behind. The air is sweet with wild phlox and clover and the last of the June lilacs. There's no one else around. Halfway down one row, I stop. Max does the same, planting his feet a short distance away. Side by side, we stare through the ruffled green treetops, over the slope of the hill, down to the swollen river.

I keep quiet. I know what I need to do next. But I'm not sure how to begin.

Or if I want to begin.

"Have you ever seen that play, *Our Town*?" Max asks, out of the blue.

"No," I answer.

I've *read* it, but I don't feel like telling him that. I don't want to give him anything that I don't have to.

"My school put it on last year, and everyone had to attend, for an English class assignment," Max goes on. "Anyway, the last scene is in a cemetery, and all the townspeople who have died over the years are sitting there in rows of chairs, quietly gazing out into the distance." He pauses, gives a little shrug. "This just reminds me of that."

I hate how hard these words hit me.

Because this boy doesn't understand. He *can't* understand. I picture my grandma Kay, my great-grandparents and great-great-grandparents, all my ancestors seated in chairs on every side of me, watching their home slipping away. And I know what they're waiting for me to do.

I stiffen my spine. The humid air hums around me.

"Max," I say, turning toward him. "I can't–"

"Hold on." He's frowning at me. Like he's already guessed what's coming.

But he's not looking into my eyes; he's looking at the side of my face, above my left ear.

I lean back. "What–"

"Just hold still for a second."

He reaches out with one hand, his fingers combing softly through my long hair. So softly I can hardly feel it. Hardly believe it. There's a muffled buzz beside my ear that grows suddenly louder, and then Max's hand lifts up, smoothly, gently, and I hear the buzzing streak away.

He smiles. "You had a wasp in your hair."

Before I know what I'm doing, before I know why, I thread my hands into the dark hair on either side of his face, my palms along his jaw and the warm, lilac-sweet air spinning in my head. And then I press my lips to his.

It's not my first kiss.

There have been games of truth or dare and spin the bottle and stupid moments at backyard parties. There was prom, a flashing dance floor and a blaring 1980s power ballad, Jake's hand sliding lower and lower on my bare back.

But this is the first kiss that feels like I thought it would.

For the first half second, Max keeps still, and that's more than enough time to flood my brain with doubt. But then he shifts, leaning closer, and his lips move against mine, and his fingers slip softly into the hair beside my face again. This time, they stay.

I feel his breath against my cheek. I feel his chest pressed to mine. I'm falling deeper into this moment, his smooth lips and his warm T-shirt and the clover and the buzz of insects in the air.

I'm falling apart.

I jerk myself backward.

"Sorry," I say.

"What?" Max closes the gap between us. "Why are you sorry?"

I step back again. I turn away, so I'm facing the river, not him, not the gold and black in his eyes. "I didn't mean to do that."

"It's okay," he says, and I can hear that he's smiling, even without looking. "I would've—"

"We had a break-in," I say sharply. Like a door slamming shut. "At the museum."

Max hesitates. ". . . You did?" He sounds surprised. Maybe something else. "Did they take anything?"

"A bunch of things. Some replica weapons, some antiques. The town founders' stuff."

"Whoa," says Max. "That's awful. I'm sorry."

I nod. And now I turn toward him. I need to see what's on his face.

He looks concerned. Mildly puzzled. Bemused. Like he can't decide which demeanor to put on.

"Do they know who did it?" he follows up. "Have they caught anyone, or . . ."

"Not yet." I fold my arms over my sweaty chest. "There's security camera footage. It's just not very clear. But it looks like two youngish guys. Wearing Minnesota sweatshirts."

I watch him closely. Was that a flinch? Am I imagining it? Is the look on his face a different kind of surprise?

Silence strings the humid air between us. I can feel it pulling me off my feet.

It's pulling Max too.

His face changes. "Are you asking if I had something to do with it?"

I fold my arms tighter. "I'm not asking anything."

He stares at me. Studying me. His mouth tugs up with a half

smile. "Do you think I've been, like, *planning* this? Casing the place? Trying to trick you into trusting me?"

I shrug. I force myself to keep my gaze on him, not to let it weaken and slide away. "You show up here. Nobody knows you or your family. You come to the museum over and over. You tell me about you and your friends getting in trouble with the police. Then suddenly we have a break-in. For the first time ever."

"Seriously?" His half smile is still there, sharp as a hook. "I also own a Minnesota hoodie. Is that enough proof to close this case?"

He gives a little laugh. A snort, really.

I almost want to laugh with him. But I've let my guard down too far already. I've been an idiot too often to make it a joke.

"Okay," I say. "Maybe you didn't have anything to do with this."

"Maybe," Max repeats.

"But it doesn't really matter," I push on. "Either way, I shouldn't have been–" I stop. Breathe. "I need to focus on the important things right now. The museum. My grandpa. Black Point Days is coming up; it's our busiest time of year. I need–I need to think about what's *real*."

He's looking straight at me. I can feel it, even though I can't quite face him anymore. "And I'm not real," he says softly.

"You and your aunt–you're just here to try to change things, and when it doesn't work, you'll disappear again. That's all."

Max stays quiet for so long that I finally take a glance at him.

His face is cool now. It's the unreadable blank from the day we met, like a page where all the words have been erased.

"Well," I say at last. "I should go. There's a ton to do for the festival."

"Sure," says Max. "I should get back to the hotel. We're tearing down some kitchen walls. Ani will need extra help."

I swallow the thought of a bunch of strangers ripping into the old hotel and square my shoulders. "Fine. Good luck."

Max turns away. He walks quickly through the rows of gravestones, the shade of the giant trees and the patches of sunlight making him seem to disappear and reappear again. "Feel free to tell the cops to come search my room, by the way," he calls back over his shoulder. "Anytime."

Then he steps into another shady patch, and he's gone.

My knees feel wobbly. I don't know if it's the thickness of the air or something else, but I sink down on a marble bench in a patch of fluttering shade and take a few deep breaths. Then I pull out my phone.

Normally I'd just send a text. But I need to hear his voice. I need to know the things he might not say with words.

Jake picks up on the second ring. *"Lucia Sorenson."*

"You sound surprised," I say, because he does. Surprised and pleased.

"I *am* surprised. I don't think you've ever called me before. I mean, you've texted me a few times, but . . ." He laughs. "It's a nice surprise. So. What's up?"

I take another breath, choosing the best path. The one that's least likely to smack me straight into a wall. "We had a break-in at the museum on Monday. The night of my birthday party."

"Whoa." His voice rises. "Like, a robbery? What did they take?"

"A few things. Important things." I brush away a mosquito that zips past my ear. "And I just wondered, after you left my house that night, did you guys see anything? I know you hang out downtown sometimes, so I thought maybe you'd been near the museum, and you might have noticed something strange."

"No," says Jake earnestly. "No, we weren't near the museum that night."

What did *you do?* I want to ask. I picture a deer's severed head, dead eyes staring up from a bloody front stoop. I picture a bonfire. Bullet wounds. A pool of blood dribbling from the bed of a pickup truck.

What did you do?

I shift my tone. "So . . . ," I begin. Casual. Knowing. "Did you three maybe leave something at the hotel that night?"

I expect him to deny it. He'll either sound sincere or like he's lying.

Instead, Jake bursts out in a laugh.

"Okay," he says, still chuckling. "Yes. Maybe. But that's all it was."

The picture in my mind—the bodiless deer head, the mess of flesh scraps arranged around it—suddenly seems silly. I've made a nightmare out of a joke.

I try to laugh too. "What do you mean?"

"I mean, we just thought it would be funny," Jake goes on. "We didn't kill the deer or anything, just so you know. It's not hunting season. But Colton's uncle does deer processing, and he had this fresh roadkill buck, so we got some stuff from him. We actually tried to be respectful with that whole part. We had a fire, gave it part of the carcass. You know—to honor this place. And then we . . ." He laughs again. ". . . Got creative."

"Were you trying to scare them off or something?"

"If it scares them, that's on them." Jake's voice gets suddenly firm. "You know they're not going to last here anyway. They'll just mess everything up and then disappear again."

"Yeah," I say softly. "I know."

"Hey," says Jake. "I'm really sorry about the break-in. If I knew anything about that, I'd tell you. You know that, right?"

"Yeah," I say again. "I know you would." I take another deep breath of the sticky air. "I'd better go."

"Okay. See you."

For a few minutes, I sit on the cemetery bench, holding my silent phone in my hands. Insects hiss and swirl around me.

I saw the security video. I already knew the thieves weren't from here. And now Jake and Colton and Kyle have an alibi—a gross one, yes, but a totally believable one, too.

But Max . . . I don't know what he did that night. Who he was with. I don't know what he feels about me: the girl who just threw herself at him and kissed him out of the blue, the girl he'll leave behind as easily as he'll leave this place when he goes back where he belongs.

My thoughts split as neatly as a halved apple. I can put my trust in the people I've known for my entire life, or in the one person who I don't really know at all. The choice is so clear I don't even need to make it.

I slap a mosquito against my forearm a second too late. It leaves a red smear of my own blood on my sweaty skin. I wish I could smash the memory of that stupid kiss just as easily, flatten it into a sting and a fading red stain.

Wiping the blood away, I get up and head back down the hillside.

April 17, 1986

Matt—

I think I'm in trouble.

I did some stupid things. What else is new, right? But I'm not so stupid that I don't know they're stupid. Since I went to the cops yesterday and told them about the missing woman's stuff up in the attic, I've barely been able to think straight. I feel like a narc and an idiot and a traitor and a sitting duck, and I don't know which one I actually am.

Maybe if I could think straight, I could tell.

Okay. I'm going to try to write everything in order, so I don't start sounding even stupider.

Today, at lunchtime, that cop from the station came in. He was in uniform and everything. He doesn't usually come in at lunch. But he just sat down at a table and asked Jeanne for the lunch special. I told her, "I'll get his coffee!" so I'd have an excuse to get over there. I thought maybe he was going to ask Jeanne or Maeve some questions, or maybe he wanted to talk to me again. I brought his coffee, and when no one else was nearby, I asked, "Have you found out anything yet? About that missing woman?"

He said, "We're looking into it."

And that was it. He barely even glanced at me. Then Jeanne came over with his hotdish, and he looked right at her and gave her a big smile, and I heard them talking about the weekend, and how high the water was getting, like everything was totally normal.

I don't know, Matt. Either I'm making a huge thing out of something that barely mattered twenty years ago, or everybody else already knows something, and I'm the only one who can't see it. Neither one feels good.

After the supper shift, I headed out to the woods. I'd heard Bruce and a couple of other townies in the hotel bar talking about a bonfire out in the bluffs tonight, off County H. I figured if any of the guys knew about that missing woman, I might be able to get it out of them when they were sloppy drunk.

Plus I didn't want to be in this old hotel anymore.

It's a pretty long walk all the way from the middle of town to the corner of County H, and it feels longer in the dark. But I made it. I found my way down the dirt roads, using the moonlight, following the sounds and the lights of a couple parked trucks in the distance, until I finally got to the river bottoms.

A little crowd of kids was there. I didn't get a good look at anybody, though, because it was really, REALLY dark out there except for the bonfire, and because the minute I got close enough to make out faces—I don't know. Something happened.

I was just walking up to the edge of the group, and they'd all been talking and drinking, but the second someone spotted me, everything changed. All their eyes moved to follow me, even though their bodies went totally still. Nobody even raised a can to drink anymore. It was like when a pack of dogs sees you. On alert.

So I froze too. I was still way back from the flames, but I'm sure they could all see my stupid, scared party-crashing face.

I took another quick glance all around, and I saw Bruce, and that scrawny drunk kid, and camo guy. But there were a lot of other faces too. And none of them looked friendly. So I looked straight at the bonfire instead.

And Matt, here's the weirdest part.

There was something in the bonfire.

Not wood or brush or trash or anything else you would normally burn. Something that looked like an animal. A big animal. Maybe a cow or sheep or something. I saw hair. I saw legs. I saw bones.

And before you think I got freaked out by some people having a barbecue, that's NOT what this was. You don't cook out by throwing whole animal corpses into the fire.

I saw this stuff, Matt.

They saw me see it.

Still, nobody talked to me. Nobody moved. They just stared at me with those wolf-pack eyes until I backed away.

So I pretended like I was just out for a totally normal walk in the woods, and I'd just accidentally found this totally normal party, and now I was going to get on my way. I backed up out of the firelight, and then I turned and walked straight back up the path. I wanted to run, but I forced myself not to. Things chase you when you run.

I didn't hear anybody coming after me. I didn't hear anything at all except the crackling fire until I was almost back to the gravel road. And THEN I started to run.

The whole time, I was thinking about where I should go. If there was any place that would feel safe. But the next little town is ten miles away. I wasn't going to walk it in the pitch dark. Black Point doesn't have another hotel or motel or anything. Plus, I had no money. And I sure as hell wasn't going to sleep out in the woods by myself. Jesus.

The only thing I could do was go back to the hotel, where at least I could lock my door and wait until morning.

It had felt like a long trip getting out to the bonfire, but man, it felt a hundred times longer getting back. It was so dark, and there were so many weird animal sounds from the river and the woods around me. Every time a truck drove past, I could feel the driver slowing down to stare at me, and every single time, I felt like I was going to have a heart attack.

By the time I got back to the hotel, swear to god, this old place had never looked better. The lights were still on, and some of the old guys like Les the mechanic and Officer Bjorklund were still drinking at the bar, and Maeve looked up and nodded at me. I blew straight upstairs. I wanted to be shut in my own room, where at least I could see someone coming. If anyone was.

I unlocked my door and turned on the lights. Everything looked fine. No moved ashtrays, no new stuff lying anywhere.

So I stepped inside. Right into a puddle.

There were big wet footprints across the room again, Matt. They went from the bed to the door and stopped. Like someone had been trying to get out. Or was telling ME to get out. I can still see them all over the carpet beside me. This time, I wasn't even going to try to clean them up.

That's when I did the next stupid thing. Maybe the stupidest thing yet.

I picked up the phone. I dialed the operator and made a collect call to the house.

Yeah. OUR house.

At least I remembered to say it was from Neil SCHMIDT.

Dad must have picked up. I'm not positive, because he didn't accept the charges, but YOU would have. Right? So it had to have been him.

I don't know if he put things together. I mean, it's late, he could've thought it was just some drunk with a wrong number. But he might have realized it wasn't a coincidence. I mean, that someone with the same first name as his runaway kid was calling him collect in the middle of the night.

So if he starts putting pressure on you, Matt, I'm sorry.

Please don't tell him anything. Please.

Now I'm sitting here wishing I could rewind the

last fifteen minutes. Or the entire night. Or the last few weeks. Or months. I don't know.

Between dad and the warehouse guys and the truck, I can't go home. But where else can I go?

I don't know. I don't know.

I've got to get out of here.

—Neil

11

MY BED IS TREMBLING.

Not just my bed. My whole bedroom. The old wooden floor vibrates. The windowpane rattles in its frame.

I roll over to stare at the alarm clock on top of my cluttered dresser, but there is no clock. The glowing red numbers are gone, leaving just one more black shape in a mound of black shapes. I roll toward the window instead, and all I see through the wet glass is darkness. No house lights on the hillside below. No moon. The storm has swallowed everything.

The blackness matches something inside me. I hadn't realized how much it had changed things—having someone new here, someone I didn't already know but wanted to. Now that's over. Switched off. An absence of light.

Another drumroll of thunder shakes the house. Rain pounds the roof. I picture dark water sliding down through the streets of Black Point, running over land already saturated with months of snowmelt and rainfall. Dragging our town into the river, drop by drop, grain by grain.

These floods are more frequent now. It used to be every ten, twenty years. Now it's every five. Or less. And they're not going to pull back. As much as everyone here loves to talk about the weather, they don't like to talk about what it means.

Anyway. There's nothing we can do but try to hold on.

I swing my legs out of bed and hurry to the bathroom. The light switch, which I hit by habit, does nothing but give a soft click. Power is out, of course. This happens more and more too.

I find the toilet and the sink in the pitch dark. Good thing every inch of this house is as familiar as my own heartbeat. But when I step back out into the hallway, I see something that isn't familiar. A swimming red-gold light that floats up the old wooden staircase.

I head down the steps.

Grandpa is probably up, rechecking the seals on the windows, making sure every latch is locked.

But I don't find Grandpa. I find Mom.

She's in the dining room, a cluster of candles burning on the table, checking the windows—just like Grandpa would normally do.

I glance along the hallway into Grandpa's wing, where his bedroom, bathroom, and tiny study are. His bedroom door stands open. But he's not here.

"Where's Grandpa?" I ask.

Mom startles. She turns to face me, candlelight fluttering across her old blue robe, her tired face.

"Oh, Lucia," she breathes. "The thunder woke you too?"

"I guess." I step toward the table and push one candle farther away from the edge. "So, where is Grandpa?"

"He's out."

"Out?" I repeat. The needle of fear hits fast. "In *this*?"

"He's with the guys," she answers. "I'm sure they're fine. Probably just down at Les's."

"Have you checked? Did you call him?"

"He doesn't like being hovered over. You know that."

Mom is right about this, at least.

There's another house-shuddering boom. The wet windows flash. For an instant I can see the rain-soaked street, the dimmed hulks of neighbors' houses staring back at ours, hunkered down, clinging on.

"Aren't you worried about him, though?" I ask Mom.

She takes a long breath before answering. "He knows how to take care of himself, whether or not he actually does it." She double-checks the lock on one front window. "He'll be fine."

Turning away from the window, she steps past me, toward the kitchen. "Want some hot chocolate?"

"How are you going to heat it?"

"Oh. Right." Mom gives a faint smile. "Want some chocolate milk?"

We head into the kitchen, each carrying a candle. Their uneven lights wash the walls like high waves.

Mom goes to the fridge. It opens, dark inside, silent. Everything feels wrong.

"Grandpa was still here after dinner. Until I went up to my room," I say, because I can't let it drop. "Why would he go out in this?"

"I can't say," Mom answers. She thumps through the cupboards, taking out cups and spoons. "He's got his reasons, I'm sure."

"Did he walk, or take the car, or . . . ?"

Mom sighs. She seems worn out by my questions. "I think Chuck picked him up."

I point at the window, rippling with a sheet of rain. "Chuck shouldn't be driving in this."

"Nope. Probably not."

Mom sets down the cups of chocolate milk. She seats herself in the chair across from mine and busies herself with a napkin, a spoon, never looking straight at me. There's something in her face that makes the fear inside of me spike higher. Something off.

Suddenly, she looks straight at me. She raises her eyebrows and puts on a smile. The change is so sudden I lean back in my chair.

"You know, you could invite Max over for supper sometime," she says. "Sometime when there's not a whole party going on. Might be more comfortable."

"Thanks," I tell her. "But no."

"No?" Her eyebrows go even higher. "Grandpa and I could make ourselves scarce too. We wouldn't be helicoptering around you like—"

"No," I say again. "He's leaving soon. And there's some stuff about him, things I've learned. I don't think I'll be spending time with him anymore."

"Oh," says Mom mildly. There's a pause. "What about that Jake Meier?"

I look at her through the flickering light. "What about Jake Meier?"

"Do you see him sometimes?"

"God, Mom. You and the Oldies." I put my head on one hand. "We go to the same school. We have some of the same friends. He was at my birthday party. Yes, I see him sometimes."

"You went to prom together," says Mom.

I muffle a growl. "We went to prom *in a group*, Mom."

"Well, Jake was the one in your picture."

I snort-sigh. Lean farther back in my chair. "Why are you asking? You want me to end up with Jake Meier?"

"No," says Mom, in a new, firmer tone. "I want you *not* to end up with Jake Meier."

I blink at her. "What?"

"I don't want you to end up with any of those Black Point kids who are never going to leave this town."

"Mom—"

"Lucia," she cuts me off. "You need to get out. I'm telling you. You need to get out of here."

I turn my cup around. Candleglow slides around its rim like a curved blade. "We've had this argument a zillion times already. You know what matters most to me."

"Lucia. I am telling you." Her voice sounds sad now. Or maybe hopeless. Because she already knows I won't listen. "I'm *asking* you. To get out."

A blast of wind rips along the hillside. I hear it hiss and roar between the houses, through the whipping branches of the trees. Another shock of lightning flares.

Mom turns toward the windows. "Maybe we should head to the basement."

"No." I push back from the kitchen table. "I'm fine up here."

Leaving my candle behind, I head up the staircase to my room.

April 18, 1986

Goddammit, Matt. GODDAMMIT.

I should have seen it sooner. I should have started walking out of this place the second I walked in. I should have freaking CRAWLED. Because it's been right here. The whole thing. The ghosts. Those guys with their fires in the woods. The water every time. Goddammit.

It's too late now. And you'll probably never even see this, but I'm writing it anyway, because there's nothing else I can do.

Okay—stop. Just the facts.

I was going to get out tonight, Matt. Walk. Hitchhike. Whatever it took. I had a big plate of food down in the kitchen, cause I didn't know when I'd eat again, and then I worked the supper shift, and it was packed tonight—half the town seemed to be here, Bruce and all those townie guys—and then I came upstairs and I threw all my stuff in a plastic bag. I was going to wait until everyone was gone or in bed and then sneak down, take a little cash from the register, and get out.

So it was really late, and it was pitch dark, and I crept down the stairs.

But they were still there. In the dark hotel bar.

Just waiting.

I dont know if they saw me. I couldnt really see them. But I'm pretty sure it was Jeanne, with a few younger guys.

I heard them talking.

He's a runaway. Never even told us his real name. Knows too much now, either way.

I just stood there, frozen, on the steps, but my hands were shaking. My stupid plastic bag gave a rustle.

And they all went silent.

They heard.

So I ran back upstairs and shut myself in my room. I was going to climb out the window or sommthing, but it's too high and then I was going to use the phone, but it didnt work and I looked down and the cord under the desk was cut, and my hands are startng to feel all numb now Matt

and then I noticed the wet footprints all around, the lipstick on the cigaret burning by the bed, the white beads on the bedspread, likefrom a weddng dress.

They were trying to tell me all this time, Matt

So ~~I run~~ I ran back to the door, cause now I was just going to make a break for it, run anywhere, even though my legsare barely working ether

but the door was locked.

From the outside.

They locked me in here.

you see it, right? I should hve seen. But don't call the police here, Matt

Theyll know

that stupid plate of supper on a tray I should have

they were telling me, matt

they were all warning me

Don't

it's too heavy now

12

THE STORM DOES ITS DAMAGE, BUT BLACK POINT HOLDS ON.

The next morning Grandpa and I walk downtown, taking stock. Grandpa had gotten home, perfectly safe, after the worst of it had passed, and he had a perfectly reasonable excuse, too: There was some glitch in the museum's new security system that set off an alert, so after meeting up to fix it, he and the guys had had a chat over at Les's place, which had turned into a marathon card game. When the storm hit, they'd all just decided to wait it out.

"You could have brought me along," I tell him as we head down Redtail Avenue on foot. "I need to know about museum security."

"Of course you do. We'll fill you in on everything. But, Luce," Grandpa adds with a grin, "you wouldn't have wanted to be there last night. Because you are a *terrible* poker player."

I give an indignant tut. "I am not."

"You have a dozen tells."

"I do not!" I argue, even though I'm laughing.

But both of our laughs stop when we reach the edge of Main Street.

The big Black Point Days banner that's strung across the street each year has torn loose from its cords and trails to the sidewalk on one end, soaked and shriveled. Wind and rain have ripped down the swags of artificial flowers on each lamppost. A shallow river runs along the gutter on the far side of the street. I know without saying it aloud that if the water is that high out here, it's filling the basements around us. Maybe seeping into the first floors too.

And Riverside Park is underwater.

Except for the flagpole and the very top of the swing set poking out of the blue-brown waves, you wouldn't know there was a park there at all. Even the towering cottonwoods and box elders look suddenly shrunken, their bodies submerged, branches dragging in the waves like waterlogged clothes.

Maybe Grandpa is right about me not having a poker face. I'm sure he can see the worry on mine. But his just looks empty. Tired and empty.

We walk back uphill, along Main, past one of the high-water posts that stands on either end of downtown, where the levels of historic floods are marked with notches and little white numerals. Most of the year, the post is as tall as a telephone pole. Now it's just a stump sticking up out of the water.

Grandpa nods at the post. Only a handful of years are still visible above the sloshing brown. We haven't reached the level of 1965, the flood of record, or 1880, which I guess people called "the flood of the century." But we are creeping higher.

He lets out a breath. Then he says, "Guess we'll need to add another notch."

But by Friday morning, things have slid back toward normal. Or as close to normal as they can come.

The parade has been rerouted to Second and Third Streets. The fireworks will go off from Hilltop Park, instead of over the water. The craft fair and food tents have been moved to the municipal lot up on Third. The frontage is still gone. Basements are flooded. Low-lying roads around town are out, and the water is still rising. But the Oldies and I are up in the big parking lot behind Swede's Garage an hour before the museum's opening time, putting final touches on the parade float.

Black Point Days will happen in spite of the storm, in spite of the founders' stuff being stolen. In spite of everything.

Around me, the Oldies are chatting. Sometimes even laughing. The sounds of repairs—hammering, chain sawing, fallen tree limbs being cleared away—join their voices in the morning air. It should be comforting. But just now it feels fragile. Tenuous. Something else I have to hold on to.

"Looks good," says Grandpa, nodding at the fresh red paint I'm adding to the dragon's head. "You've got a knack for this. I think you missed your calling."

"Yeah. By about a thousand years."

Grandpa laughs. He doesn't look too bad this morning: a little tired, but not ashen. I've made sure that I'm the one doing the heavy work, dragging downed branches, picking up storm-blown trash. Trying to keep him safe.

Chuck climbs down from inside the longship, where he's been replacing a broken plywood oar.

"All right," he says, coming to stand beside Grandpa. "We're ready to roll."

They study the longship appraisingly. Grandpa nods. "Better than ever."

"After the parade, we should take her out on the river for a little ride," Chuck goes on. "Frankie, you ready to row?"

The Oldies make this joke every year.

"Sure," I tell Chuck, forcing a smile. "Duane and I will row, you bring the life jackets."

"Rowing?" Duane speaks up from the far end of the ship, where he's patching a scrape in the side. "I was planning on bringing my rod and doing a little fishing."

"Fine. I'll row all by myself." I shake my head. "I *am* the only one who does any work around here."

The Oldies all laugh. Then Grandpa starts to cough. The cough lengthens, turning wheezy and harsh, making him hunch into himself. The Oldies halt, watching. I jump down from the crate.

"Are you okay, Grandpa?"

"Fine," he chokes, still coughing. "Fine. Just a tickle in my throat."

I shake my head. "You've been out in the damp too much."

"Aw, the damp doesn't give you a cough," says Grandpa, straightening up at last. "It gives you *fevers*."

I sigh.

He grins, putting a big hand on my shoulder. "I'm fine, nurse. Just fine."

Reluctantly, I head back to my crate. The Oldies go on talking behind me. Les launches into a fishing story I've heard a hundred times before, and that I'm sure—or I hope—I'll hear a hundred times more.

"Lucia," says a low voice.

I stiffen.

The voice came from the other side of me, far from the circle of Oldies.

I glance around the quiet Swede's Garage lot.

Between two old trucks, several feet away, I spot a crouching shape. A familiar shape.

Max.

My heart jerks.

He's stooping there, pressing close to the side of a broken-down Dodge Ram, like he's trying not to be seen.

"Hey," I say back.

A rush of feelings strikes me. Confusion, surprise, distrust, and on top of them all, something stronger and brighter. Something like happiness. But I'm not going to reveal that. Not to anyone. I keep my face as still as I can.

Max's gaze slides past me to the Oldies. They're still huddled together, not noticing us. "I need to talk to you," he murmurs.

In the right tone, this might sound personal. Like he's come to apologize, or confess, or like he needed me for some other reason. Like maybe we're going to talk about that idiotic kiss in the cemetery. But it isn't the right tone. His voice is low and taut. And his eyes, which keep flicking past me toward the Oldies, are nervous. Cold.

"Why?" I ask, taking a small step toward him. "What's going on?"

"I can't explain everything here." His eyes dart beyond me again.

My guess was right. Something must have happened that has shoved him back in my direction. It isn't about me at all.

I plant my feet. "What is it?"

His voice drops even lower. He speaks fast. "We were tearing down a wall between the kitchen and the old hotel office. And there were a bunch of old letters inside the wall. Like someone slid them into a vent or something."

"Okay," I say slowly.

Max meets my eyes. "You have to see them."

I frown at him. "Why? Who are they from?"

He shakes his head. I'd started to recognize his amused face, his joking face, his carefully blank face. But I've never seen him look afraid before. "You just—you really need to read them."

I hold out a hand. "Okay. I'll take them."

"No," says Max quickly. "At the hotel."

I let out a sigh. "We're getting ready for the parade. There's still tons of stuff to do for Black Point Days, and the museum is—"

"Please," Max cuts me off. His voice is low but sharp. *"Please."*

I throw a glance back at the Oldies. They're still absorbed in their discussion. I think I see Duane send a look back at me, but it's so quick that I can't be sure.

I sigh again. "I guess I could come for a little while."

"Thank you," Max breathes. "Just don't tell anyone where you are. Don't tell them anything. See you at the hotel." He turns away.

And he doesn't walk. He runs.

I make up some excuse about needing to drop by the drugstore for sunscreen and promise I'll head to the museum as soon as I'm done. The Oldies wave me off, going back to their discussion as I hurry away. A coal of dread in my chest goes with me, small and painful and stubbornly present, as I head down Falcon Avenue to Main Street.

Max throws open the hotel's front door before I can even knock.

"Come in," he says. "Quick."

He slams and locks the doors behind me.

There's no one else in the lobby. It's still a mess of stacked furniture and plastic sheeting and industrial power tools, but no one is working anymore. The place feels deserted. Beneath the fading smells of sawdust and oil, there's the stronger scent of damp. Mustiness. Mud. The whole basement could be full of water. Rotting from the inside out.

"Where's your aunt?" I ask.

"In the Cities for the weekend," he says shortly. "She had to pick up some things. I stayed here to let the workers in. But with the flooding, they're all gone too." He nods toward the staircase. "The letters are in my room."

I follow him up the steps.

His room looks just like it did on my first visit: narrow bed, dusty landscape painting, papers and cords and T-shirts strewn everywhere. Max clears a spot for me on the bed. He waits until I sit down. Then he opens the drawer in the tiny desk and pulls out a bunch of yellowed papers, all folded in three, held together with a rubber band.

He sits beside me. I feel the warmth of his arm against my side and the twitch of his muscles under his skin—tension or nervousness or impatience. He hands me the letters. His hands are shaking.

"Are you all right?" I ask.

"Not really." His eyes don't meet mine. "So, these letters were in the office wall. I'm the only one who's read them. They were folded and bundled up just like this."

"Okay," I say slowly. He's suddenly so broken and strange, all the anger I'd felt toward him—the anger and distrust and wariness—fizzles. At least for a moment.

"I don't know if—" Max breaks off. "I just— You seem like the person to show them to." He taps the topmost letter. His movements are jerky. "That's the first one. Start there and read to the end."

I unfold the pages. They're the kind of paper you'd tear out of a school notebook, with the fringed edges where a wire spiraled through. They feel brittle, delicate. They're all covered in scrawly blue ink.

March 29, 1986

Hey Matt,

Once I can buy some stamps, I'm going to mail this to Alicia's so dad won't see it. At least he won't if you're smart and leave it there instead of bringing it home. I'm guessing Alicia will read it too (HI, ALICIA!), so I won't write anything too embarrassing. About myself. You're fair game, though. Ha ha.

I keep going, and after a while, I forget where I am, and whose arm is beside mine, and everything except for the story in the pages. A story I should already have known.

13

I READ ALL THE LETTERS. TO THE VERY LAST PAGE.

Then I reread the last words again.

they were all warning me

Don't

it's too heavy now

But there's no ending. Stories need an ending.

And that's what this is. A story, something that makes you believe it, even though you know it isn't true.

Max watches me. I feel his gaze pressing hard against the side of my face.

"So," he murmurs, like someone might overhear. "What do you think?"

Confusion and bemusement swim around inside me. And underneath them, there's something else, something that's trying to push its way to the surface like some huge, hideous bottom-feeding fish lunging for the air.

But I shove that back down. I don't want to see it. I don't want to look it in the eye. Even though I know it isn't real.

"I think . . ." I take a breath. "I think this kid was messed up."

"Messed up," Max repeats. "Like—crazy?"

"Like clearly drunk or something, in that last one at least." I shift the stack of brittle pages. "I mean, he was in all kinds of trouble already. He was a runaway. He could have been a pathological liar. Or on drugs. He was obviously having delusions, or hallucinations. Whatever."

Max pauses for a moment. "You told me about the hotel ghosts yourself, though," he says. "You said everyone around here knows the stories. It's not like he was making that part up."

"Well, yeah, but—they're *stories*."

I halt, looking down at the papers again. In the last half hour, I've read so many of Neil's words, in his own scribbly handwriting, that it almost feels like I know him. But I don't. Not like I know this town.

Yes, I know about the ghosts. And of course I believe the part about the bonfire out at the Bend, the one that Neil stumbled upon in the dark. Maybe he made something out of nothing, or maybe it actually was some kind of sacrifice, an offering to nature or the gods, a tradition like the one Kyle and Colton and Jake were carrying on. Maybe. But the rest—it doesn't make sense, even if I recognize the pieces. It's like someone turned a map upside down.

"I'm not saying *everything* here is a lie," I say. "Maybe this kid—Neil—did see a ghost, or something weird or supernatural or whatever. But then it's like—it's like he made a bunch of connections that weren't really there."

Max is studying me now. "So," he says, "you know a lot of it is real. The details about this place, the hotel, the town." He ticks things off on his fingers. "The stuff in the attic. All the people he mentions by name, like Jeanne and Maeve. And 'Frank, the history buff'—that's your grandpa, right? But you think the bad stuff is imaginary."

"You think it isn't?" I stare at him. "I mean—what do you think he's suggesting? That someone or something around here is *murdering people* every couple of decades? You think that part is *true*?"

He stares back at me. The gold flecks in his dark eyes look different to me now. Like something shattered. "People here would have good reasons to cover it up. Especially if it had to do with their kids." He gives a rough shrug. "Of course the town would cover it up."

Indignant heat flames through me. "*The town* would cover it up? Like we're all one big evil entity? And it can't be the same 'kids' every time anyway, because the stories go back for, like, a hundred and forty years." I throw one hand up. "It's just ghost stories. Ghost stories and one kid's letters." I pick up the stack again. "Just think for a second," I say, shaking the papers so their frayed edges rustle. "You found these walled up in Jeanne Hansson's old office, right? Why would Jeanne have kept them there? If they were proof of something that needed covering up, why would she keep them at all?"

"I don't know," says Max. "But the Hanssons obviously didn't mail them for Neil, either. They kept them. Like all that stuff in the attic. The same stuff we've seen, and that Neil describes, in every single detail. The bride's dress. The bird-watcher's stuff. The old magazines and jewelry and lipstick that must have been Carole what's-her-name's. And I think–" He stops for a second, voice dropping lower. "I think there's a box up there that belonged to Neil. I've seen it. T-shirts. Jeans. A couple of 1980s paperbacks."

"So?" I shove the letters out of my lap, onto the bedspread. I don't want to touch them anymore. "This kid was a runaway. He made a bunch of dumb choices. He said so over and over. He probably made some more dumb choices, and then ran away again."

Max gets to his feet. "Yeah. Maybe. Fine." He whirls around, facing me from a few steps away. "But if some totally broke teenage kid ran away, why wouldn't he at least take his stuff with him?"

This throws me for a moment. And I hate that it does.

"Have you tried looking this up?" I ask, trying to keep my voice smooth. Rational. "Have you looked online?"

"Of course," Max answers. "But we don't even know Neil's actual last name. We know some kid named Neil from Madison ran away and might have disappeared back in 1986. Pre-internet." He shakes his head. "There's nothing. There's nothing about the other disappearances either. Not even about Carole, and we know that was in the papers back then. There was just one mention of the ghost bride in some article about haunted Wisconsin inns."

I shake my head back at him. Even though it makes me feel dizzy. I get to my feet, too, and face Max head-on.

"Listen," I say firmly, each word a brick I'm mortaring into place. "There's no way this is true. I would *know*. This is Black Point. Everyone here knows if somebody cheats, or if somebody's a drunk, or if somebody has one little pot plant under a grow light in their closet. There's no way I wouldn't know about this. I *know* these people."

"Right," Max says, more quietly. "You all know each other. You're all related. You all protect each other."

A bitter taste floods my mouth. Now my words are more like nails than bricks. "You knew I wouldn't believe this. Right? Even though you don't know me, or this town, or—"

"Shh," says Max.

I stiffen. "Did you just shush me?"

"Listen," he whispers. His eyes are focused, but not on me. He's staring straight at the closed bedroom door.

"What?"

"Just listen," he whispers, his voice even softer now.

I catch hold of the words that want to storm out of me, yanking them back. And I listen.

Nothing.

The hotel is quiet. It might as well be underwater.

And suddenly that quiet, the rows of empty rooms above and below us, all the hollow places where people used to move and sleep and breathe, seems eerie. Heavy. Airless.

"I don't hear anything," I breathe.

Max steps to the door. Carefully, he turns the knob and pulls it open.

There's no one in the hallway beyond. But now, drifting through the open door, I hear it.

Jazz music.

It's faint, slightly tinny, like it's being played on an old phonograph.

"You hear it now, right?" Max asks.

And I can tell he's asking as much for himself as for me. He wants to know this is real.

He can see the answer on my face.

We stare along the row of closed doors. The music could be coming from behind any of them.

I still want to refuse this. To look for other explanations. Tell myself a different story. But the music keeps playing and Max and I stand, frozen, until the song ends, and the last note dissolves in the damp air.

I close my eyes. I'm trying to dig up the right thoughts, but the waves keep pushing against me, getting deeper all the time.

"You know who we should talk to," I say aloud.

Max turns quickly toward me. I see gratitude in his eyes. Maybe because I'm making a plan. Maybe just because I used the word *we*.

"Yeah," he says. "Let's go."

14

THE INTERIOR OF MAEVE'S SHOP IS AS STUFFY AND DIM AS ON our last visit. A layer of mud has joined the smells of incense and litter box. Together, they're as thick as a wall. We practically have to push our way inside.

Maeve stands behind the glass display counter, arranging driftwood around the trays of polished rocks. Her pale eyes swing toward us.

"Hi, Maeve," I begin. "How are you?"

She doesn't answer this. And it's clearly Max she's speaking to when she says, "Knew I'd see you again before too long."

Max manages a mechanical grin. "Yeah. Still here."

Maeve nods once. She drops something into the tiny pot of burning incense that's adding its smoke to the murky air.

"Have things been pretty busy?" I ask. "With Black Point Days this weekend and everything?"

I'm not sure why I feel the need for small talk. Maybe the odder this whole situation seems, the more I'm compelled to act like everything is normal.

"Every year," Maeve says, which I guess counts as an answer.

"Will we see you at the parade on Saturday?" I press on.

Maeve doesn't even seem to hear me now. Her snowy eyes home in on Max.

"Living in that place is getting to you, isn't it," she says abruptly. It sounds like a statement, not a question. "Too much of the past stuck in there."

Max looks slightly unsteadied, like an invisible hand has pushed him forward.

"That's actually why we're here," he begins. "I found something else. In the hotel." He takes the stack of letters out of the sketchbook where he's tucked them. "These were inside the office wall. Letters from a kid named Neil who stayed and worked there in 1986."

Maeve's face is hard to read, but one thing I know I don't see on it is a single twitch of surprise. "What are you wondering?" she asks.

Max keeps the letters in one hand, proving that they're there, but not letting them go. "Just—if you can tell us about him. Whatever you remember."

Maeve's eyes drift to the letters. There is a quiet beat. "He was a fast talker," she answers. "Hard worker. Good at getting himself in trouble."

I glance from Maeve to Max to the letters in his hand. For a second, it almost feels like Neil is standing here between all of us, a skinny kid in a stained T-shirt and stonewashed jeans. My heart starts beating faster. There's a prickle of cold, soft as a breath, on the back of my neck.

"So, what happened to him?" Max asks.

There's another beat.

"He left," says Maeve.

"I guess we're really wondering . . ." Max throws a look at me and amends his words. "*I'm* wondering if something might have happened to him. Because in these letters, he describes a bunch of things that were going on around the hotel. Strange things."

Maeve doesn't move.

"He saw things, like wet footprints, a trailing wedding dress, cigarettes burning in a locked room," Max continues. "He thought the place was haunted."

"He's not the only one to have seen those things," says Maeve.

I feel another prickle of ice.

"No, I know," says Max quickly. "I've heard the stories. But then he found that stuff in the attic. The same stuff I asked you about before. He realized those boxes each matched with one of the ghost stories. The woman in white. The drowned man. The lipstick lady. And then he found out that the lipstick lady had probably been a woman named Carole Harran who was last seen here in Black Point in 1965."

Maeve still doesn't move. Her eyes, on Max, are as cloudy as ever. She almost looks tired. Like she was expecting all of this, and now she's just waiting for it to end.

I'm waiting too. But I'm not sure what I'm waiting for anymore, what I'm hoping will emerge. Max is wrong. All of this is absurd, as fragile as an unraveling ribbon. But I need to hear someone else say it.

Maeve isn't speaking, though. Not yet.

"So this kid, Neil, went to the local police," Max presses on. "But they didn't do anything. Then he was going to get out of town, but his truck had broken down, he had no money, nobody to call. He mentioned some weird bonfire in the woods, hearing some locals whispering about him and locking him in his room. And then the letters just stop. So it seems like he—like he might have disappeared too."

Max's voice stays steady until the final words.

Hearing him put the story together this way, bit by bit, pulls my stomach into a fist. It's still ridiculous, though. There's another explanation. I wait for Maeve to give it.

But, of course, she's Maeve.

Her eyes drift down from Max's face. "You're not wearing it."

Max blinks. "What?"

"The bag I gave you. The stone and the rune. Do you have it in your pocket?"

"Oh," says Max. "No. I guess it's back in my room. At the hotel." He glances at the letters in his fist. "So, do you know anything about Carole Harran? Or about what happened to this Neil kid after–"

He's drowned out by a roar from the street outside as several huge trucks roll past. I catch a glimpse of metal posts, folding ladders, a wood chipper. More cleanup and setup for the festival.

Now Maeve's face shifts. Her eyes tighten.

"All this," she mutters, and I wonder if she's even talking to us. "For that."

I clear my throat. "You're not a fan of Black Point Days?"

Her gaze slices to me. It's like she's truly looking at me for the first time since I stepped inside. My skin goes suddenly numb.

"Did you ever wonder why there aren't any Angstroms in this town?" Maeve asks.

My brain scrambles to follow hers. "Angstroms?"

"There have always been some Hanssons," she goes on, with a tiny gesture toward herself. "Plenty of Lundbergs. A few of you Sorensons left." She pauses, still looking hard at me. "But no Angstroms."

I push Maeve's fragments together. Angstrom, Lundberg, Hansson, Sorenson. The town founders. The ones whose possessions are still missing. Maeve's ancestors and mine.

"I guess . . . I hadn't ever noticed that," I say slowly.

Maeve stares back at me, not speaking.

"Does that have something to do with . . . anything we've been talking about?" I ask. I'm trying not to sound offensive, but it can be hard to do that with Maeve and still have an actual conversation. "Are you saying–"

But Maeve's eyes fly away from me, back to Max.

"You should wear that pendant," she tells him. "All the time."

"Um . . . ," says Max, looking dazed. "Okay. But can you just tell us–"

The shop door swings open, letting in a burst of noise and hotter air. A cluster of out-of-town visitors–an older couple and a family with two small kids–steps inside. I see them all blink around, rocked back by the smells.

Maeve gives Max and me one more look, her gaze floating between us. "You should stay together," she says.

"Oh." I stiffen. "We're not–"

I glance at Max sideways.

"Not together," he finishes.

Maeve gives a little headshake, like we've missed her point. She turns to her new customers. "Good morning," she says. "All used paperbacks are two for one today."

I look at Max again, then at the plate glass window. More people are heading toward the door.

"I suppose we should go," I say.

Maeve doesn't glance at us again.

I lead the way out into the late June sun.

Max and I halt on the sidewalk for a second, staring at each other. There's more to say, I suppose, because nothing feels settled. Nothing is clear. I should have known that Maeve would give us more questions in place of any answers.

But I'm not going to have this—or any—conversation with Max in broad daylight, on Main Street, with Black Point Days preparations bustling all around us.

"Down here," I tell him, heading along Main to the end of the next block.

Here the tight-packed buildings of downtown end and the land slopes toward Riverside Park. Of course, right now there is no park, only more river. But there's still the very end of a dirt road that runs down to the submerged frontage, a sheltered spot between the last Main Street building and a half-sunk grove of cottonwood trees. I turn onto that road. Main Street cuts out of sight behind us. Below us, the river slides, high and dark.

I press my back to the brick wall.

"Okay," I say, turning toward Max. "We can talk here."

Max places the letters inside the cover of his sketchbook. "So," he starts. "She was obviously hiding something."

I want to laugh. I shrug hard instead. "She was just being Maeve."

"She wouldn't tell us anything," Max argues. "But she definitely knew. She just kept changing the subject."

"She always does that. Her brain doesn't go in straight lines."

He shakes his head. "She knows something. I'm sure."

Now I *do* laugh. "So, what's your theory? You think Jeanne and Maeve Hansson were criminal masterminds? Two weird but nice old ladies who made pie and hotdish and hotel beds all day long were secretly running a serial killer ring?"

Max takes a step sideways, like he's not sure how close he should stand to me. "It's not just a coincidence. All the stories around that hotel. The people who've disappeared."

"Yeah. Because nobody stays in a hotel forever," I answer. And I realize that now I sound a lot like Maeve.

"It's a pattern."

"A pattern?" I shoot back. "Seriously? Let's go through the things we actually *maybe* know." I tick them off on my fingers, just like Max did in his room an hour ago. "There's the bride, in the 1870s or 80s, who everyone says killed herself. There's the bootlegger from the 20s, who probably got offed by the mob. In the 50s, some bird-watcher drowns while working along a giant river; what a *weird* coincidence." I throw one hand toward the wide water. "In 1965, there's a woman who's fleeing from her boyfriend. And in 1986, there's a runaway eighteen-year-old boy. There *is no pattern*. It was forty years between disappearances, if you want to call them that. And then thirty, and then fifteen, and then twenty-one. And they were all different kinds of people—"

"Not locals," Max breaks in. His voice is low, but quick and hard.

"Right," I concede. "There'd be a lot more *facts* if they were locals."

"And they were all staying at the hotel."

"Thousands of people have stayed in that hotel!"

"Exactly," says Max. "Easier for one to go missing every now and then."

"Oh my god." I let out another laugh. "This isn't an Alfred Hitchcock movie. If that were happening, people would have figured it out."

"Not if the right people covered it up."

The right people. Black Point people. My people. He's accusing all of us. My whole battered, flooded, barely hanging on town.

I throw out both arms. "Why?" I demand. Max leans back, eyes narrowing. Their gold flecks go dark. "Why would they cover it up?" I rage on. "What is the point? Why would any of this happen? There's *nothing here*! There's—"

While I'm mid-sentence, Max turns on his heel and strides away.

I see something worse than fury in the hard line of his body.

He's giving up on me.

"Fine!" I shout after him. "Just leave! Get out of our town!"

He doesn't halt or glance back.

"And leave our founders' stolen stuff when you go!" I add even more loudly, barely caring if anyone hears.

Max has already disappeared around the corner of the building.

I stand alone on the dirt drive, fuming, hands clenching. Turning my back to Main Street, I stare out over the swollen water. So much is hidden beneath it now: roads, train tracks, entire buildings. The wreckage of the old Catch of the Day Café slumps in the distance, its broken rooftop floating above the blue-brown waves like a tiny island.

I glance toward the flood-marker pole a few yards off. The

water has climbed even higher. A handful of hash marks hang above the surface: At the top, *1965*, the highest the waters have ever reached. A few inches below that: *1880*. Just a bit lower, *1952*. *1986*. Then *1997*, *2001*, *1927*.

Black Point has withstood all of this. It's held on. I can hold on.

I look at the numbers again.

1965. 1880. 1952. 1986.

1965. Lipstick Lady.

1880. The bride.

1952. The bird-watcher.

1986. Neil.

I stand there for a while longer. Until my eyes burn and my head aches. For so long I almost expect the flood waters to rise up and cover me, too.

15

THE REST OF THAT AFTERNOON FEELS PATCHY.

The museum swirls with a tide of out-of-town visitors. All the post-break-in repairs are finished, but there's plenty left to do for the festival. I should be focusing on my work, or on the last-minute prep for the parade, but my brain keeps dragging me back to those last moments in the street with Max. To those notches on the flood pole.

Each time it happens is like a long, slow blink. Like I've had my eyes shut long enough for the whole world to change around me. I greet visitors. Blink. I sell tickets. Blink. I stare around at all the cases full of familiar and precious weapons, ancient knives and swords and axes and spears, and everything looks suddenly less familiar.

My roots in this town should be wide and deep enough to hold me steady. But the earth beneath me is eroding. Slipping.

I'm not sure how long I can keep myself straight.

1965: Lipstick Lady. *1880*: The bride. *1952*: The bird-watcher. *1986*: Neil. A little farther down the pole: *1927*. The bootlegger. *1997* and *2001*, two more notches on the flood pole, float in my head, unattached to names or stories. But the hotel was closed by then. Maybe there are stories for those years too. They just don't have a place to stay.

And now. Our own flood year. The water creeping higher.

"You all right?" says a quiet voice from behind me.

I spin around.

Duane sits in his usual chair behind the front desk, carving a Dala horse from a piece of pine. I've been standing stone still at the register for long enough that someone else would notice—at least, someone who knows me as well as Duane.

"Yeah," I tell him. "I'm fine."

"That trip to the drugstore took a long time," he says mildly.

"Oh. Yeah." I push back from the counter. My knees feel stiff. My stomach squeezes. "Tons of out-of-towners around. It took forever to get my stuff, and then I stopped at the gas station, which was packed too." I'm rambling, nervous, going on too long. "The streets are full of people who don't know where they're going. Plus all the Illinois drivers tearing up the River Road."

Duane grins. "Makes me miss giving speeding tickets sometimes."

"I'll bet." I half smile back.

I study Duane for a moment. His bald head, his soft belly, his big, rough, woodworking hands. I think of all the tiny wooden animals he whittled for me when I was small. I think of all the times he's plowed our driveway or walked his snowblower down our sidewalks, without ever saying a word about it.

This is who I can trust. My own people. Not Max, some outsider I've known for a couple of weeks. This town, my family: This is what I truly know.

There's no way, I tell Max again, in my head. *There's no way.*

"Hey, Duane," I say. "Do you know anything about a woman named Carole Harran?"

A twinge of guilt chases the question. And maybe something else, something between worry and fear. Max asked me not to tell anyone. But I didn't make him any promises. I don't owe him any; not the way I owe the people right here. And I have nothing to be afraid of. That's what I tell myself. Nothing at all.

Duane's face stays perfectly clear. Not a twitch or a blink. "Carole Harran," he repeats.

"Yeah," I say, when he doesn't go on. "I guess she went missing from around here back in the sixties?"

Now Duane gives a slow nod. "From the Chicago area. She was running away from her boyfriend, if I remember right."

"That's her." There's a zing of relief in my chest, like when you've lost your keys and then you find them in your own pocket. No one was hiding this old story, trying to cover it up. Of course not. It had only been out of sight. Just like every other hotel ghost story: The truth was made of time, and weather, and the kinds of loss that happen anywhere.

"Do you remember anything else about her?" I ask. "Carole Harran?"

Duane shifts the half-carved horse from palm to palm. "Well, I was just a kid myself when all that happened. I heard she'd been staying here at the hotel, and then she was gone, and state police were looking for her. That's really all I know."

"So, you don't know what happened?"

"If I did, I hope she'd be found by now," says Duane with a sad little smile. "But in situations like this, it's usually the most obvious answer. Ninety percent of the time, it's the boyfriend, or the husband. In this case, I guess there just wasn't enough evidence."

There's a burst of noise from across the floor as a big group of visitors laughs at something one of them said. Duane's blue eyes slide to them, then back to me.

"Where'd you hear about her?" he asks.

"Oh. Just . . ." I shrug one shoulder. "Around town, I guess. Someone I was talking to."

Duane's eyes are still on me. "Was it that Max kid?"

There's an extra little pulse in my heart. I tug on the key dangling from the silver chain around my neck. "Maybe. I guess it might have been."

At this moment, the front doors swing open, letting in a fresh rush of tourists. I sell tickets, and Duane hands out brochures, and after that group, there's another, and another. Duane and I don't talk about Carole Harran anymore.

But we don't need to. His words reassured me. There's nothing here; definitely not the story that Neil was trying to tell. Not the story Max believed.

There's no way.

Time stutters again, and I'm standing beside a rack of spears, gazing across the museum floor like it's a big aquarium and all the people drifting through it are fish in summer clothes. Then Grandpa's voice snags my attention.

He's a few yards to my left, near the sword display, speaking to a group that has formed a half circle around him.

". . . A gift to the gods. Or to nature itself," he's saying. "It's unlikely that something as valuable or as honored as a sword would just be *lost*, in a location like that. The placement in a lake or a bog had to be deliberate. Probably as part of a ritual or a sacrifice. Swords had names, identities, destinies that spanned many human lifetimes. That's why there are legends like the Lady of the Lake."

I've heard him give this talk a thousand times. It's not the words that hook me. It's his voice. It sounds raspier than usual. Wheezier.

I take a step toward the group.

Grandpa's skin is pale. A thin sheen of sweat glazes his forehead.

"Like I said, these five are replicas," he goes on. "But you can see examples of some much older metal smithing in our collection. And I'll be right nearby, so just holler if you've got other questions."

He makes it to the end of the sentence. Then he turns his face away, stepping quickly aside as the visitors drift on, oblivious. But I grab his arm.

"Grandpa," I whisper. "Are you okay?"

"Yeah, yeah," he whispers back. But his arm feels heavier than usual in my grip. "Just need to sit down for a minute."

I steer him toward the front desk.

Duane glances up from his carving. He jumps silently to his feet, grabbing Grandpa's other arm and moving him toward the chair. Grandpa sags onto it.

"You sure you're okay?" I ask. "Do you need anything? Should I call the doctor?"

"No." He waves a hand. "I'll be fine. A little lightheaded for a second. That's all."

I study his face. His drawn, grayish face. "I should at least call Mom. You don't look–"

"Lucia." Grandpa claps a hand over mine, which is still holding him by the arm. "I'm all right. Heartburn isn't a heart attack."

"We shouldn't have gotten lunch at the Badger Hole," says Duane guiltily.

"You guys," I scold. "Aren't you old enough to know better?"

"You know what you can do?" Grandpa says. "You can grab

me a glass of cold water. Don't worry," he adds when I hesitate. "Duane is right here to watch me while you're gone."

I hurry to the back office. I find a clean glass in the cabinet and fill it from the water cooler.

By the time I get back to the front desk, Grandpa is on his feet, and he and Duane are laughing about something, and my heart starts to slide back from my throat down to the notch in my chest where it belongs.

"Thanks, nurse," says Grandpa as I hand over the glass. He leans back toward Duane. "Well, you remember what happened that time when Les forgot to get a trailer hitch, and we ended up having to push that damn longship all the way down the parade route?"

They both laugh again.

"This is easier to fix, at least." Grandpa turns to me. "Les forgot his clothes for the parade tomorrow morning," he explains. "Would you run them down to his place?"

"Sure," I say. "Right now?"

"We're closing up in ten minutes anyway." Grandpa hands me a heavy brown paper bag. Inside are the folds of a linen tunic, a piece of faux sheepskin, leather straps.

"Be sure to give him a hard time for forgetting them," Duane adds as I head toward the doors.

I step out into the early evening sun. Les's house isn't far, just a few blocks down the hillside on Falcon Avenue. It's an easy walk. Or it should be. But summer weekends in Black Point mean invasions of motorcycle clubs, boat travelers, vacationing couples. With the festival on top of everything else, these will be the wildest nights of the year.

The flooding doesn't seem to have quieted things down. Live music blares from the Badger Hole—I can hear the laughter from their back deck and the off-key blues rock screaming from inside. A row of out-of-town Harleys fills the block from Lou's Café to the post office, and knots of buzzed visitors cluster outside every open bar door.

It's a good night to get out of downtown, at least if you're a local. Most of the high schoolers are getting together up past the cemetery, at the little park on the bluff. There will be a keg, bottles of brandy and vodka, the usual. Cara and Bailey are going. I might head up there eventually. But I'm not really in the mood. I don't want to look around at the faces lit by a bonfire and think about which ones will be gone next year. Or imagine a kid in 1980s stonewashed jeans standing beside me.

A bunch of middle-aged bikers in too-tight black T-shirts have gathered on Second near the Badger Hole, smoking and laughing. I walk past them, fast, keeping my eyes straight ahead. One of them whistles. Another shouts something I can't make out. There's a laugh. I hear the word *jailbait* and then another burst of laughter.

I hate that my cheeks get hot. I hate that I don't turn around and flip them off. I hate these outsiders coming into our town, thinking they can make this place theirs, even for a weekend.

I walk faster.

I pass an out-of-town couple having a loud fight near The Blue House B&B, and a bunch of guys who graduated from BPHS when I was a freshman standing around someone's lifted, NRA-sticker-plastered pickup. Another group brushes by me, heading the opposite direction. I hear a voice say, "What's up, Lucia?" and glance over just in time to see a knot of guys slouch by, all of them bleary eyed and loud and obviously already drunk. Jake Meier throws me a grin over his shoulder. Behind him are Colton and Kyle and someone else I recognize. Someone with black hair and a T-shirt with graffiti on it instead of a sports team's name. Someone who stumbles over a crack in the sidewalk, clearly the drunkest of them all.

I spin all the way around.

It's Max.

He doesn't even notice me.

Because he's wasted. He's wasted, and he's hanging out with the guys who sent death stares at him through my entire surprise birthday party and who then left bits of bloody deer carcass on his front stoop, getting drunk with them just a couple of hours after he accused every single one of us of being part of some horrible conspiracy.

Confusion and surprise swim through me first. Anger lunges after them, swift as a shark.

What a hypocrite. What a *liar*. Telling me I'm the only one here who he can talk to, telling me that I should distrust my own home, making me question people who've known me ever since I was born. And now here he comes, too drunk to be bothered by any of it himself anymore.

Behind these thoughts lurks another one. The thought of the teenage townies in Neil's letters, gathering around their bonfires, trading their secrets. Burning things. Things that were once alive. Instinctively, I wipe my hand on my leg, still feeling the sticky blood that pasted Jake's palm to mine.

But Max clearly isn't thinking these thoughts. Who knows what he's thinking, or why he's acting this way, or what he really believes?

Not me.

Because I don't know him at all.

I turn away and walk even faster now, my steps so hard they should leave cracks in the concrete.

16

LES'S PLACE IS THE SECOND ONE IN A LINE OF OLD ROW HOUSES with brick facades and tiny front porches. I'm still fuming from my glimpse of Max, and I pound on the door a little harder than I need to. Les throws it open for me.

"Hey there, Luce," he says, grinning. "Come on in."

I step into Les's living room. The place probably hasn't been redecorated since the late eighties, when his wife packed up and left. The furniture is worn but comfy, the walls a faded shade of peach. The place smells of cigarettes. I've been inside many times, usually on visits with Grandpa for a round of cards or a cup of coffee, and it's always looked exactly the same—not a single new picture on the walls or a single plastic plant in a different place.

"I've got your parade clothes for tomorrow," I say, holding out the brown paper bag.

"Ah. Thanks." Les sets the bag near the end of his couch. He glances at my face. "You mad at me for forgetting my stuff? I suppose I could have walked the parade in my bathrobe instead. It looks almost like sheepskin."

"No." I thaw my face into a smile. "No. It's just—the crowds. Some other stuff."

"Sure." Les nods. "Hey, I know what will help. I've got some of that good pound cake from the bakery. And I just made fresh coffee. Come on in and have a seat."

"No, I should really . . ."

I trail off. I don't know what I should do. Except try to forget everything Max ever said or showed me. Except try to forget Max himself.

"Oh, I won't keep you long. You can still get out and have some fun tonight." Les gestures to the little round table with two chairs off to the side of the front room. "And there's something I wanted to talk to you about. Take a seat."

One chair—the one angled toward the TV on the other side of the room—is Les's usual spot, so I take the other. A stack of car and truck magazines spills across the tabletop.

Les heads down the short passage into the kitchen at the back half of the house. I hear him humming nasally to himself. There's a slosh of coffee, a clink of plates and forks.

"Here we go." Les comes back, plunking down a plate and mug carefully in front of me. "If your mom minds that you've ruined your dinner, just tell her to blame me."

I smile at him. "I will."

The wedge of pound cake from the bakery is topped with crackly dark chocolate, but I'm not feeling hungry. At least the coffee smells good.

"I put in a little cream," says Les, seating himself and nodding at my mug as I lift it. After years of sharing a table at Lou's Café, he knows exactly how I take my coffee. He knows pretty much everything about me.

This has always felt right. Comfortable. Loving.

But for some reason, tonight, it makes me prickle.

I wonder what it would be like to walk, slightly drunk, down a street where everyone around you *didn't* know who you were. Where you could disappear. Be someone new. Take your coffee a different way.

I take a sip. Even with the cream, the coffee's bitter. It's probably been a year since Les has washed out his pot.

"Taste all right?" he asks.

"Yeah, it's fine," I say. And because he looks worried, I take another sip.

"So. I'm glad we've got the chance to chat for a minute without your grandpa right nearby." Les takes a forkful of his cake. "Not that any of this is a secret. It's just tough to talk about some things in front of him. You know."

"Things like what?"

Les finishes another bite of cake before he goes on. "Well, you know—we all know—that he's not doing so great." He shifts in his chair. "I mean, we all hope he'll be around for a long time to come, telling everybody what to do. Lecturing us about the right names for the parts of an old sword." He half grins. "But we want *you* to know, and I mean me and Duane and Chuck and your grandpa too, that if something happens . . . We're all going to be right here to help you." His voice gets gruffer than usual. "That's what would make Frank happy. To know things are going to go on, just the way they should. The museum. This town. Your family. We'll carry on. Okay?"

I meet his eyes. "I know you will. Thanks."

This should feel comforting too. I'll have help from the people who know me best. We'll keep everything the same, in honor of Grandpa. It's what I've always wanted. But suddenly this changelessness lies on my shoulders like a weight.

I take another drink of coffee. The bitter taste fills my mouth.

"So," says Les, sitting back. "I haven't seen that kid from the hotel around lately."

There's a teasing edge in his voice now.

I snort. "He's still around. I just saw him out on Second Street, with a bunch of guys from school. Looking smashed."

Les shakes his head. "Everyone gets a little wild at Black Point Days." He glances at my mug. "You want a warm-up?" he offers, even though it's still half full.

"No," I say. "I'm fine."

But I'm not fine. I feel too warm. Too weighted. Like the

future hanging on me is pulling on my limbs, making them heavy and numb.

My mind flits to the letters again. To Neil's words. His numb legs and hands.

Les watches me as I pick up the mug. But this time I just set it back down.

"You upset about that kid? Max?" he asks.

I don't answer. My mind's too full.

Les shakes his head. "Don't be. He's one of those fly-by-night types. He and his aunt, I'm telling you. Here today, gone tomorrow. And, hey. You're too good for him anyway."

I try to smile. My stomach feels wrong. My heart is beating fast.

"We weren't *together* or anything." I force the words out. Maeve's statement—*You should stay together*—pushes itself inside me in their place. Advice.

A warning.

"Good," says Les. "I'd hate to see you feeling sad when he disappears again."

I look into my coffee mug, then back at Les. I trace the lines around his brown eyes. The outline of his dark gray hair. What is wrong with me, that suddenly he looks different? My heart thumps harder.

What is wrong with me?

"Finish your coffee so you can get out there and join your

friends," says Les. "Cara and Bailey and everyone meeting up on the bluff tonight?"

"I think so." I cut off a small bite of cake, but don't eat it. I'm stalling now. My thoughts move like mud. If I was just being my usual honest, comfortable self, what would I say?

I need to say it. This is my chance.

"Hey, Les," I begin, trying to sound as light and unsuspicious as I can. "Do you remember a kid named Neil who worked at the hotel for a little while? About thirty years ago?"

Les isn't like Duane, with the perfectly blank face. I see a flick of his eyes. A little change in his mouth.

"Thirty years is a long time," he answers. "Neil, you said?"

I venture forward, like feet on a balance beam. "Yeah. Eighteen years old. He had a broken pickup truck. He said you were—you were going to fix it."

Les frowns. "He said?"

"In a letter we found." My tongue is dry, heavy. "At the hotel."

Les leans back in his chair, mug in both hands. "My memory's not as sharp as it used to be. Heck, I just forgot my clothes for tomorrow. I'm not going to remember some kid I did a little work for back in the eighties." He gets to his feet, grinning self-deprecatingly. "I need a refill, and a quick visit to the boys' room. Give me just a minute."

He heads down the little passageway, taking his coffee mug with him.

I didn't say it was the eighties.

I said thirty years ago. That would mean early nineties, rounding down.

But Les knew.

He knew when Neil was here.

He remembers.

He lied.

And if he lied, what else–

Who else–

My head swims. But it's not just the thoughts inside anymore, I'm almost sure.

Something is wrong.

The bathroom door clicks shut.

I could run. I could run, and Les would know that something was up. Or I could stay here and try to learn something more. To be sure.

I need to be sure.

Fast as I can, I pick up my coffee cup and creep to the kitchen.

Les's half-full mug is sitting on the counter, near the coffee maker. There are no pill bottles around, nothing medical or dangerous, as far as I can see. But I need proof before I'll believe that Les, someone who's been like an extra grandfather all my life, would do something like this to me.

I slosh the contents of Les's cup into the sink, tip most of my coffee into his mug and the rest down the drain–I hope I'm matching the amounts–and pour myself a fresh half cup from the pot. My hands are shaking, rubbery. I barely manage not to spill. I creep back down the passage to the table just in time to hear the bathroom door creak open.

New thoughts hit me. Maybe Les didn't need to use the bathroom at all. Maybe he was sending someone a message, planning a next step. Because whatever Les is doing, whatever he's done in the past—he didn't do it alone. In Neil's letters, it was a group of local kids gathering in the woods. It was some younger guys plus Jeanne Hansson, whispering in the hotel bar on Neil's last night. It was—

Les sits down across from me again, holding his own steaming mug. "Topped myself off," he says. "Sure you don't want some more?"

"No," I say. "I'm good."

I take a big swallow of the fresh coffee.

Les watches me closely. He swigs his own drink.

I brace for a change in his face, a moment of doubt when the bitter taste strikes. But a lifetime of smoking must have dulled his taste buds. There's no change.

So maybe I'm wrong. Maybe I'm being crazy. Maybe there was nothing to notice in the first place.

I take another big drink.

Please let the caffeine keep me sharp, I pray. *Please don't let the weight filling me get any stronger.*

"You know," says Les, drinking too, "your grandpa might not say it enough, and the rest of us definitely don't, but we sure are grateful for you."

Sudden guilt shakes me. "Grateful?" I get out.

"You're a good one, Luce. You're going to be here, keeping things going, making sure everything's all right. So this place doesn't go downhill." Les's voice is tender. He drinks again. "You're what this town needs. There's always got to be somebody here who understands. Who carries on the traditions. Who keeps things running the way they should run. That's what we've all tried to do. And our families before us."

He takes another long swallow.

My chest is starting to ache from the thud of my heart. I need to keep him distracted until whatever might be in the cup takes full effect. And I need to stay awake. Aware. Until I can get away.

"You're a good one," he says again. He's slurring his words now. "Not like some kids. Not like that kid at the hotel."

His head is starting to nod.

"Max?" I prompt.

"That Neil," says Les, his tongue slow. "Just trouble, some kids. Not from here anyway. Would've just . . . messed everything up . . ."

Les's half-lidded eyes lock on me. I see something in them connect.

He knows. He realizes what I've done.

I jump to my feet, so quick and clumsy that I almost knock my chair over. Its legs thump on the thin carpet. Les stands up too. He lunges forward, reaching across the table. Just before he can grasp hold of me, he loses his balance, catching himself with one arm on the tabletop.

My heart thuds with fear. But I can't be afraid of Les, this skinny old man who I've known since the first day of my life. It's wrong; it's impossible that there would be something like this hidden here for so long. Something I wouldn't have believed yesterday. Something I wouldn't have believed an hour ago.

I've backed out of his reach. But Les isn't moving now. I don't know if he *can* move. He stands, hunched over, braced on one bent arm, breathing hard.

My chest floods with pity. But he would have done this to *me*, I remind myself. He'll be all right. He has to be all right.

I grab him by one bony upper arm and tug him upright. Then, fast, before he can grab onto me in return, I wheel him around and push him backward. He falls onto his saggy striped couch.

His eyes slide shut.

He's still breathing. Loudly. Heavily.

I stumble-run back down the passage to the kitchen. I lean over the sink, sticking two fingers down my throat. Maybe I can get the tainted coffee out. I gag, but nothing comes up. Instead I splash my face with cold water and drink a long stream straight from the faucet.

Maybe it's the water, or maybe it's the terror, but I feel a shred more awake as I run back down the hall, past Les wheezing on his couch, and out the front door.

17

I FLY ACROSS LES'S FRONT PORCH AND POUND DOWN THE SIDEWALK.

I'm not sure where I'm going. What I'm doing. At first, I just run, trying to breathe and stay upright, trying to push back the misty, tilting feeling that fills my whole body. Every time my head starts to clear, the dizziness swims back again.

Please stay awake. Please think.

Think.

Why would Les drug me?

To get me out of the way.

Out of the way so they can do what? And who are *they*?

In my mind, fragments spill and cluster. And suddenly something takes shape.

Generations of local kids gathering around bonfires in the forest, laughing, telling stories, passing on their traditions.

Generations of kids taught by their ancestors—like Kyle's grandpa Bruce. By father figures like Les. The kids who are just trying to hold on to this place, where their families have lived for so long. The ones who will never leave. Like Kyle. Like Colton. Like Jake.

Like me.

For a second, I think I'm going to throw up after all.

I stop, leaning one palm against the sun-warm brick of the old bank building on Second Street. Clusters of people brush past, not pausing. I probably look like one more kid who's had too much to drink.

Now what?

What do I do?

Who do I tell?

Who can I trust?

There's only one name I can think of.

And he might already be in their clutches.

I wrench my head up, scanning faces as they pass. Even the familiar ones look strange now, distorted and out of scale. Strangers' faces barely look like faces at all, just collections of features, staring eyes, bared teeth. No Max anywhere.

When I can move again, I turn toward the river, rush down Redtail Avenue and onto Main Street.

The sidewalks here are crammed. The reek of smoke and mud and high water is everywhere. I dodge knots of people, skirt the crowds near every shop and bar. Most places stay open late for Black Point Days. But Maeve's shop, I notice as I rush past, is already closed.

I race all the way down Main to the hotel.

Its heavy double doors are locked. I pound and pound and pound, not caring if everyone on the street notices me.

No one answers. On the other side of the papered windows, the lobby looks dark.

He's not here. So where is he?

Panic adds itself to the blur in my bloodstream like sulfur to a spark. My vision wobbles. My legs feel like rubber.

I trip my way back down the stoop, almost landing on my hands and knees on the sidewalk. Two hands catch me just in time.

"Whoa," says a loud voice.

Smiling blurrily down at me is another familiar face. Jake Meier's face.

"Jeez, Lucia." He grins. "Getting messed up pretty early, huh?"

"No," I say. "I'm not . . ."

But my words come out in a drunk's slur.

"You been drinking alone? You should've hung out with us." He puts an arm around my shoulders, holding me up, pressing me tight to his side. His Black Point Wrestling T-shirt smells like beer and cologne. "We're going to get some stuff from Kyle's house and then head up the hill."

I blink past Jake, at the other faces waiting behind him. Kyle and Colton. No Max.

"Weren't you guys hanging out with that other kid?" I push the words out as precisely as I can. "Max?"

Colton snorts.

"Not really." Jake gives a little shrug. "He was hanging out with *us*."

"Okay, but–"

"Yeah," Kyle speaks up. "He just ran into us and followed us around town for a while."

"He did? So was he–was he okay when you–" My knees wobble. Jake holds my shoulders tighter. It's almost nice: being held up, taken care of. But *almost* nice isn't really nice at all. Jake wraps an arm all the way around me, his thumb rubbing my arm. Like I'm his. Like he expects me not to resist.

The other guys laugh.

"He was wasted," Colton scoffs. "He kept talking about ghosts in the hotel. He was totally freaked out."

They all laugh again. At the ghosts. At Max.

Max, who might not have been drunk at all. Who might have been swaying on his feet, just like me, drugged and scared, hoping to find someone who would believe him. Someone who might keep him safe. And instead he found these three.

What did they do with him?

There's a burst of noise from up the street as more motorcycles pull into the Badger Hole. A stream of drunk strangers jostles by. The town's packed, and still nobody notices. Nobody sees.

I try to straighten up on my own numb legs, but Jake's arm holds me still.

"Come on," he says. "We'll get the party started."

"Wait." I pull back. "Where is he now?"

Jake's face hardens. "That Max kid?"

"Didn't see where he went," says Kyle.

"Yeah, he just staggered off after a while, talking to himself," Colton chimes in. But these could easily be lies. A story they came up with together. "Seems like kind of a freak."

"Why?" asks Jake, his wrestler's arm strong and too snug around me. "Why do you care where he went?"

I can't possibly put all the right words together. Even if I could, I can't let them out.

"Forget about him," says Jake, half steering, half lifting me up the sloped street now. "Let's go have some fun."

"Max," I say aloud. They ignore me, pulling me along. "Wait. I have to find him. Where–where did he–"

There's another nearby roar.

It's not a motorcycle this time. I hear the thump of a car door and then a voice.

A woman's voice.

"Lucia."

For a second I think it might be my mom, and a flood of new feelings ripples through me. Relief. Embarrassment. Fear. She'll understand. She'll believe me.

She has to.

But the shape that steps onto the bleary sidewalk in front of me isn't my mother. It's broader. Gray haired. Still familiar.

Maeve Hansson's pale hands wrap around my arms.

"I've got her," she says to Jake and Kyle and Colton.

Without arguing, the guys back off. I watch them disappear into the blur.

Maeve steers me toward her car.

"Max . . ." I think I say aloud.

Maeve places me in the passenger seat.

"I know where he is," she says, quietly, before she shuts the door.

18

The evening already feels like a dream: the squashy sense of time, the slippery way pieces slide and stick together, the impossible things I've heard. But tearing down the highway in the front seat of Maeve Hansson's ancient blue car, with Maeve flooring it in the driver's seat beside me, I wonder if I'll ever wake up at all.

The sky beyond the windshield streams with darkening colors, fuchsia and orange and violet. The river beside us glimmers. We're roaring north, away from the noise of town. My head is heavy. I wrench it around, bracing it on the neck rest, until I can see Maeve's profile.

Max, I remember.

Maeve is taking me to Max.

Maeve knows where Max is.

I blink, and it seems to take ten seconds for my eyes to close and open again.

How does Maeve know where Max is?

Maeve senses me staring at her. Without turning toward me, and without taking her left hand off the wheel, she reaches for a metal thermal cup.

"Here." She puts it in my hands. "Drink."

The last thing in the world that I want now is more coffee. Even the thought makes my guts turn. But I am thirsty. So thirsty. I want water. I want to drink glass after glass, and then I want to lie down in a clean, empty bed and close my eyes and make all of this disappear.

"I don't . . ." I get out the first two words. But that's all.

"Drink it," says Maeve sternly. "It's tea. It will help."

I put the slot of the cup to my nose and inhale. I smell herbs, maybe. Something spicy.

"What . . ." I try again. "What's in it?"

"Turmeric. Red clover. Ginger." Maeve shakes her head slightly. "A few other things. You need it."

How could Maeve know what I need? Because she's psychic. Maybe. Or because she knows a lot more than she's said.

She notices me hesitating, the cup wobbling in my hand.

"Nothing that will harm you," she says, and both her voice and her eyes are steady enough that I believe her. "It should help you wake up."

I take a tiny, cautious sip. The tea tastes strange, too many warring flavors at once. But I don't catch any bitterness underneath, not like in Les's coffee.

Les.

A fresh surge of fear hits me.

How long will Les be asleep there, on his saggy couch? And what will he do when he wakes up?

"Drink," Maeve commands. Then, suddenly, she reaches over and tilts the cup into my mouth. I can't help but take a gulp of the warm liquid, spluttering so it dribbles down my chin.

"Those guys had him," I say when she lets go and I can lower the cup again. "Max. Jake and the others . . ."

"I know," Maeve says.

"You know where they took him? What they . . . what they're going to do with him?" My words are still coming sticky and slow. "Where are we going?" I force out, as clearly as I can.

"Not far."

"Is he still okay?"

Maeve doesn't answer.

My mouth and brain still don't fit together. Even though my thoughts are starting to clear, my body feels weighted, slow. It can't catch up.

"Just like Neil," I manage. "He figured it out. And they knew that he knew."

Maeve's eyes stay on the road.

"Whatever they did to Neil . . . Will they do it to him, too?"

I swallow. My mouth tastes like a strange blend of flowers, ginger, clay.

"Do you remember what Marina Lundberg did for a living?" Maeve asks.

The words swoop at me out of the blue, like a diving raptor. Trying to follow Maeve's thoughts is exhausting. Even when I'm not full of fog.

"Chuck's wife?" I blink. "She was a pharmacist."

Of course I remember Marina Lundberg, smiling at us from behind the counter at Black Point Drug. Chatting with Grandpa whenever he and I would stop in to pick up a batch of his medications. Sometimes even making deliveries to the house when I was little and Grandma Kay was really sick.

"Pills," I whisper, almost to myself. "Pills to make someone sleepy, or . . ." I swallow again.

Maeve doesn't nod, but her chin rises slightly. "Makes things quick. Easy."

Easy. The word worms through my stomach.

Easy to get rid of someone. The thermal mug shakes in my grip, and a wave of reddish tea spills over my hand. It burns.

Maeve flicks the turn signal, and we slide off the highway onto a narrow road. Woods surround us on either side; woods and ribbons of low black water. The sky above the trees darkens further.

"All the stuff," I say. "In the hotel. It was all there. For someone to find." I try to sit up straighter, bumping against my seat as the road twists, shoving the thermal mug into a cupholder. "Just like Neil's letters." It takes effort to string the words together. "He wrote it all down. But somebody . . . Someone hid them."

Maeve doesn't reply.

We've turned off the narrow road onto a track I don't recognize. The woods grow denser still. Bracken scrapes the car's sides. We bump down a small hill into a flood stream of water. There's a splash as it catches the car and sprays up around us, spattering my window. I wonder if we'll even make it through. But Maeve pushes the gas, and we surge forward, up another incline.

"So who—who kept the letters?" I push on. "Who hid them in the wall?"

The car moves down another short slope into a patch of sweeping branches. Maeve puts it in park. "I did," she says.

Cold washes through me.

"You?" I turn to look at Maeve's profile, both familiar and strange in the sunset light. I've known this person forever.

But I don't know this person.

You can know someone your whole life and not know them at all.

"Why . . ." My voice croaks. "Why did you put them there?"

"They belonged there. In that place," says Maeve. "I knew that someone would find them one day. The right person, the right time."

She pushes open her car door.

Before getting out, she grabs something from the back seat. Something in a bag that swings and clanks.

"Come along," she says to me.

Her tone is firm. The only steady thing around me.

I shove open my own door and stagger out. The evening is still warm, but there's a cold edge to the breeze now. Birds are quieting. Insects buzz in the dusk.

I want to ask more questions, hundreds of them, but too much is happening at once, and my brain can't hold on. New thoughts slip and crash. I can't put the fragments back together.

And the only connection, the only thread that runs through everything, is Maeve.

She owned the hotel. She hid Neil's letters in its walls. And in that very last letter, when Neil thought he saw and heard Jeanne plotting in the hotel lobby, maybe it wasn't Jeanne at all—maybe it was Maeve, her younger copy.

The thought rocks me on my feet.

Between cousins and customers and former employees like Kyle's grandpa Bruce, Maeve has ties to every person in town. Her family goes back, and back, and back, through droughts and floods and disasters, all the way to the founders. Somehow—maybe because she truly is psychic—she knows things that no one else could know.

And she knows where Max is right now.

My knees give out under me, and I lean against the side of the car, trying to breathe.

Meanwhile, Maeve heads into the trees.

I don't know where we are. I don't know where we're going. I still don't know where Max is. There's no trail, but Maeve seems to know exactly where she's headed.

I fumble in my pocket for my phone. I'm not sure who I'll call, or what I'll say. How I can explain. It doesn't matter anyway. When I stare down at the screen, there's no signal.

Without turning around, Maeve says, "Don't bother. It will never work between the bluffs way out here."

My stomach twists tighter. She knows I'm cut off. No way to call for help. My fingers are still clumsy and numb, and I just barely get the phone back into my pocket.

There's nothing else to do. I lunge after her.

Maeve climbs downhill, through the undergrowth, then up over a ridge, down into another marshy hollow. Crickets chirr. Something winged, maybe an owl, flaps through the dimness above me. I can't see the forest clearly, but I feel a tiny bit more stable than before, like the blur in my head is holding still at least. Maybe that tea did help. Or maybe it's the cooling air. The quiet. The smell of the water getting stronger and stronger.

I stumble over a fallen log, but Maeve moves ahead steadily. She knows just where to step.

As I'm getting up to shuffle after her, in the shadows beside us, I catch a hulking shape. At first I think it's an old deer blind. Maybe an ice fishing shanty dragged here and left to rot. But as I stagger nearer, I see that it's not a building at all.

It's a truck.

An old, rusted-out pickup truck.

Its license plates are missing. Its fenders are gone too, stripped off along with every other useful part. With all the scratches and rust it's hard to tell what color it used to be. I trip again, catching myself against the truck's gritty side. Through the glassless window I can see a front seat littered with dirt and dead leaves, a couple of sun-bleached cassette cases on the floor.

I crane in to look closer. The key dangling from my neck clunks against the truck door.

Metallica, reads the paper in one cassette case. *Mötley Crüe*, says the other. My heart stills.

Neil's truck.

Left here. *Hidden* here.

I shove myself backward. My hands shake. My skin rushes with ice.

Maeve keeps moving onward, into the trees, as calm and steady as if she hadn't seen the truck at all.

Or as if she'd seen it many times before.

Oh god.

Maybe Max isn't here at all. Maybe it's all a trick, another lie, and now I'm lost here, alone with her in the woods, where I can't even make a phone call.

A few yards ahead of me, Maeve halts. She looks back.

"We're getting close," she tells me.

My legs won't budge. My mind tilts between obeying her, hoping for the truth, and wanting to turn and run. Just run. Anywhere.

But Maeve is beside me again. Her free hand grasps my arm. "Lucia Sorenson," she says, as if we'd just started this conversation. "What do you know about our town founders?"

Everything is already so impossible, the question barely seems strange. "I know they came from a little village in western Sweden. I know their names. Varg Sorenson. Lars Angstrom. Jan Lundberg. Hans Hansson." I know these facts so well, I can dredge them up even through the sludge. "They traveled together to New York, then Milwaukee, then here. They lived in the big cave in the bluff for a while, until they had the . . . the resources to start building. Then they brought their families. And stayed."

Maeve keeps hold of my arm. "They didn't all stay."

"You mean . . ." I rake through the sludge again. "You mean Lars Angstrom? You said something before. Did he—go somewhere?"

Maeve doesn't answer this. She just tugs me forward, through another stand of crooked trees, along a steeper slope.

"Did you know old Norse people thought it was bad luck to save someone from drowning?" she says.

"I . . ." My brain has lost track of hers again. "I don't remember."

"They believed that if someone was drowning, it was because the water was hungry. It needed to be fed. If someone saved the drowning person, then the water would come after them instead. Kind of a cruel idea, isn't it?" says Maeve, but not as though she expects an answer. "It's an old one, though. Old ones hang on."

She tugs me downward, to a spot where the trees abruptly thin. Water glitters into view. The sky is dimming to navy, and all at once, its size, so wide and dark above us, makes me shiver. I glance around.

This is the Bend.

We've reached it by a route I've never taken before. But here we are, looking down at the familiar curve of the water, the enclosing trees, the craggy face of the bluff. The water's so high now that the mouth of the cave is submerged. It's just a darker ledge in the rock.

Maeve turns toward me. "Lars Angstrom is here," she says.

Is this another ghost story? Is it just Crazy Maeve?

I blink at her. "What?"

"The second year the founders spent here, there was a long, wet winter. Heavy snowfall. In spring, when the rains and thaw came all at once, the river rose fast. Faster than any of them expected. One day, when they came back to the cave after a long hunt in the woods, they found the water already covering its mouth." She nods toward Black Point Bluff. Toward the submerged cave. "They'd left some of their most valuable possessions inside. They had to swim through that floodwater and crawl up inside, in complete darkness, to get the things they'd left behind, before the water rose any higher. But Lars Angstrom didn't get back out."

Maeve waits. This time I don't ask any questions. My mouth feels full of mud.

"The others–Sorenson, Lundberg, Hansson–they didn't help him," she goes on. "They were giving this place what it wanted. They just watched. They let him drown."

Maeve's pale eyes stay fixed on the bluff. On the swollen black water.

"When his body floated to the surface at last," she continues, "they didn't bury him. They burned him. Right down there, at the edge of the water. Gave the ash and bones to the river." Her eyes slide over the swollen black water. "And it looked like the river was pleased. The water receded. Their little settlement flourished. In spite of diseases, storms, blights. Black Point held on. And on and on."

Maeve's hand still hasn't let go of my arm. Maybe that's good, because now it's all that's holding me up.

"Next time the water rose, the founders and their families had a bonfire. Sacrificed a calf. The town was spared from floods. A few years later, it was the same. But then came a spring when the water rose so high, it was washing out roads and pulling down buildings. Wrecking everything the founders had worked so hard for. They had their bonfire, but the river kept on rising. Right up to the mouth of the cave. So they knew it needed more.

"They chose someone," she says, turning her eyes to me. "A young woman staying alone at the brand-new hotel. She wasn't from around here. It was said she'd eloped and then been abandoned, or that maybe she was a prostitute. Either way, a girl who was bound for trouble. They chose her. They brought her out here." She looks back toward the hidden cave mouth. "They gave the place what it wanted." Maeve lets the words settle in the darkness. "Same thing the next time the water rose too high, a few decades later. And again, and again. Descendants passed the tradition along, so there were always a few old-timers who knew what to do when the water reached the mouth. They passed it right down to us."

"No. Stop." I finally form the words. "This isn't—it isn't—"

But I don't finish.

This is more than I've ever heard Maeve speak at once. It's all clear. Sequential. It makes a hideous sense. And still there are black holes in everything: deep, waiting gaps where the ground falls away. Things my mind refuses to reach for.

Maeve starts climbing downward again, toward the water, pulling me along.

"The hotel made it all easy," she says. "Strangers coming and going. No one noticing exactly where each one went. Easy to pull them in. Easy to make them disappear."

"You," I get out, as I stagger down the slope. My shoes are sodden. My legs feel weighted. But Maeve still pulls me easily behind. “You were part of it. You knew all about it. About everything.”

“I knew,” says Maeve, more softly than before. “I knew.”

She hauls me through a patch of willows. The water’s getting close.

I plant my feet, wrenching my arm back suddenly enough that she loses hold.

“Now *I* know,” I tell her. “Max and I know, so you’re getting rid of us. Right?”

Maeve faces me. The sky is sinking from navy to blue-black, but enough moon- and starlight coat her face that I can see her pale eyes staring back.

“It was time for you to know,” she says. “I closed down the hotel the minute my mother was buried. But I didn’t sell. I waited. I waited for the right time. I could see it coming. Now it’s here.”

I look into Maeve’s snowy eyes. “You mean . . . you sensed it?”

“I saw it,” says Maeve. “I saw it all. The way it had to be.” She grasps my arm again. “It’s time to end it,” she says, firm and clear, close to my face. “The water’s not getting flesh tonight.”

Her eyes stare into mine, the ice in them solid enough to bear weight, and everything I thought I knew turns over again.

“Are you ready?” Maeve asks.

I don’t know if I’m ready. I don’t know what’s coming, or what I can do when it arrives. But the seconds are sliding past with the river.

I nod.

Maeve leads me onward. Another minute and we've reached flat land. The soil below us is spongy, the rock face of the bluff looming close, cutting off a chunk of sky.

And between us and the bluff, arranged on a broken rock slab, is the wood and brush for a huge bonfire. In the dimness, I can just make out three figures moving around the pile. Even at a glance, I know none of them is Max.

"From here on, you stay quiet as you can," Maeve murmurs. "I'll keep them busy. You get Max."

"But—" I squint at the unlit fire again. "Where is he?"

Maeve points. Toward the bluff. To the pitted spot against the water, where the mouth of the cave is submerged, drinking deep.

"He's inside?" I choke. "But—he was drugged. Jake and those guys gave him something. He'll never be able to get out."

"Even if he does . . ." says Maeve. "That's what the knives are for."

I can barely feel my tongue. My whole body has gone numb. "What knives?" I whisper.

Maeve doesn't answer me.

Another voice speaks instead.

"How are we lighting it?" the voice asks. It's not speaking to us. But I know that voice anyway; it's spoken to me hundreds of times before.

But it isn't Jake Meier.

It isn't Kyle Larson, or Colton Norquist.

It's Chuck.

He's one of the figures beside the waiting bonfire, moving around its edges, adding last twigs.

"We still don't have the dang firesteel," Chuck goes on. "Are we just going to use something else?"

"Matches will be fine," says another voice.

Grandpa.

19

No.

Don't let it be him.

I'm pleading with someone or something; I don't know what and I don't know why. Because I already know that voice. I know that shape, even from a distance. Even in the dark.

"Matches will be a lot easier than fussing with that firesteel anyway," Grandpa says. I can hear the grin in his words.

Everything inside me melts. I'm mud-colored liquid inside a sack of skin. No thoughts. No bones. Nothing to move me, carry me away, to let me be anywhere but here.

Until a hand shoves me.

I stumble sideways.

"Stick to the trees where you can," whispers Maeve. "Hurry."

I'm not hurrying. I can't hurry. But somehow my feet stagger me back into the trees, where I hunch down behind their branches. My clumsy steps make too much noise.

At the same moment, Maeve strides closer to the water, her footsteps louder still. The figures beside the wood pile turn.

"That you, Les?" Chuck calls out. "Everything go all right?"

Maeve doesn't answer. She just steps closer to the unlit fire. At a distance, I see Chuck stiffen.

"Maeve?" he says. "What the heck are you doing out here?"

Behind him, the other figures have frozen too. Duane and Grandpa. I see them both now, edging out of the shadow of the bluff, into the moonlight. My stomach lurches. My brain swims. But I force myself to keep inching through the trees, moving toward the face of the bluff.

"I knew where to find you," Maeve says, loudly and clearly enough for me to hear.

Chuck folds his arms. "You need to turn around and go home."

"Always the same," says Maeve, in that Maeve-ish way, as though Chuck hadn't even spoken. "Same place. Same people. You don't have the founders' things this time, though. Guess that's a change."

"We'll manage," says Chuck.

Duane speaks up. "You aren't part of this anymore, Maeve. If you won't take responsibility, just go home and let us do what we need to do."

"Same place," says Maeve, like she's having her own separate conversation. "Same place as always. Happening more and more often now, though. Floods coming more frequently. Every few years instead of every few decades."

Maeve goes on speaking, and I go on creeping closer. I'm passing the slab and its piled branches now. Next I'll have to move across a stretch of broken rock right up to the edge of the water, and then–then–

"You really think you can keep this up?" Maeve asks. She pauses, waiting. None of them reply. "Maybe it's time to change things a little. Try a different kind of sacrifice."

Through a screen of branches I watch her reach into the bag that's been dangling from her left arm. She pulls something out. From a distance, in the dark, I can barely see it. And still, I swear I recognize it. Because I've seen it thousands of times before.

It's a knife.

A big knife, long bladed, wood handled. Centuries old.

Varg Sorenson's knife.

Chuck and Duane both freeze.

"Where did you get that?" Grandpa asks. He takes another step forward. Maeve doesn't move. "Did you buy it from those kids? The ones who broke in and robbed us?"

"I didn't need to buy it," says Maeve. "Since I paid them to get it in the first place."

There's a moment, a twitch, as if something electrical has passed through Grandpa, Duane, and Chuck all at once.

I feel it too. It wasn't Max. It had nothing to do with Max.

It was part of Maeve's plan all along.

"You–" Chuck starts.

Maeve lifts the bag and shakes it lightly. There's the clink of metal. "I've got the other knife and the firesteel right here. Lars Angstrom's compass too."

Hearing those antiques, those precious artifacts, rattling together in a sack must be driving Grandpa crazy. But he keeps his voice calm.

"Those things aren't yours, Maeve," he says. "They belong to all of us."

"They belong to Black Point," says Maeve. "Aren't you always talking about how old weapons are sacred, Frank Sorenson? How Norse people would sacrifice their precious swords to the deities of a place? Maybe it's time to try that."

"Maeve," says Grandpa.

Then there's a moment like a caught breath. I hear a splash. Small and faint. Someone shouts: Chuck, I think. Feet run into the water.

This is my chance.

I lunge out of the tree cover, running, scrambling over the craggy ledge toward the wall of the bluff. The water is so high now that the topography has changed. The ledges where Max and I stood just a few days ago, looking down at the opening of the cave, are submerged. Consumed. They hide under the water now, hard and jagged. I'm going to have to wade–or swim–just to find my way to the right spot.

Here, shadowed by the bluff, the air and water are nearly

the same color. I shuffle my clumsy feet along until the rock below me breaks, and one foot plunges down into the water. It hits a hidden shelf a few feet down. I slide down to that shelf and balance myself, waist-deep. The water is surprisingly cold against the warm June air, and I remember how huge this body of water is, that its roots stretch out to places where the snow has only just begun to melt.

Keeping my hands pressed to the gritty face of the bluff, I edge sideways. Submerged rocks knock and jab at my legs. Where the hell is the mouth? I can't see it, but I know it's here.

Hurry up, Lucia. Find it. Faster.

There—a notch in the rock, underwater, just to my left. I reach out one arm as far as it will go. All I feel is more rock. But under there, somewhere, is the break that opens upward, into a pocket of air. There has to be.

Has to be.

The voices behind me are still speaking, but I can't untangle their words now. All I hear is my pulse plugging my ears as I take a deep breath and shove my head under the water.

With one hand above the surface, clutching the rock, I sweep the other through the wet dark. I need to focus, not think about the grit and muck thickening the water, the living and dead things swimming through it, not think about everything happening around and behind me.

Yes. Here it is. A space where my arm can reach straight into the bluff.

I jerk my head up into the air, opening my eyes. Taking huge breaths.

Okay. Okay.

One more breath, the biggest I can hold.

And then back under.

It takes everything left inside me to push myself through that notch in the bluff. To believe that the gap angles upward enough to leave me a pocket of air. To think that I'll find it in time.

Eyes closed, I swim-crawl through the slippery black. I can't panic now. I can't throw my head up and swim straight for the surface. Because above me there is nothing but thousands of pounds of stone.

I grope forward. Rocks bruise my hands. My legs. I let the pain in my knees lead me upward, and I pull myself through a black tunnel until, suddenly, air—god, wonderful air—hits my face.

I'm inside.

I open my eyes. At least, I think I open my eyes. They might as well still be shut. The cave is sealed by floodwater and walled by solid rock; there isn't a slip of light anywhere. It smells musty. Sour.

I remember being here in late summer daylight, with Grandpa. How even with the brightness and breeze outside, the inside of the cave was dim and cold. How he told me we should stick near the opening, just to be safe. Now I wonder if there were things he didn't want me to see. Or sense.

Because everything here is wrong. Lightless. Lifeless. I could be sealed in a grave.

And something else is in this grave with me. I can hear a soft rasp. Like wind through a cracked wall.

"Max?" I whisper.

There's no answer. But I hear it again. That rasping sound.

Breathing.

Hands out, I creep forward. The cave floor is cold and wet. Trickles of floodwater reach up and in. My fingers brush slippery stone, sand, shards. And then something softer.

Wet denim.

"Max."

Carefully, I feel my way up his side. I find his face by touch. I can't tell if his eyes are open or closed. I can't tell if he's hurt. With my fingertips, I brush the edge of his jaw. His lips. I remember how they felt against mine, that humid afternoon in the cemetery, and I pull in a breath so hard that it makes my ribs burn.

His skin is clammy, cool but not cold. His mouth is slightly open.

He's breathing.

Oh, thank you. Thank you.

"*Max.*" I grab his shoulder and shake him. "Max. It's Lucia. Max, you have to wake up."

He gives a low groan. "Luce . . ." he starts but can't finish my name.

"Come on. We have to go."

I shove him over, onto his side. He gives a slight jerk. I hear his legs move, wet fabric against rock.

"It might be too late, but can you make yourself throw up?" I ask him.

"I thing . . ." he slurs. "Might already've taken care of that."

"Okay. Good." I grab hold of his arm. "We have to swim out of here. I'm going to pull you through. You just need to kick your legs. Okay? As hard as you can. Then we'll be out."

Max just gives another groan.

I turn around, creeping forward on my knees, until the water sloshes higher around me. With my left hand I keep a grip on Max. I reach through the blackness with my right. I have to find the mouth again. I have to be sure I've aimed right, so I'm not steering us both straight through the dark into a solid rock wall where we'll run out of air, never knowing which way is up.

I reach as far as I can. I think I've found it. I think I'm angled in the right direction.

I think.

I swallow the panic that's starting to thump its way up my throat.

If one of the Oldies–probably Duane, I'd guess–managed to haul Max into this place and then get back out again, I can do it too. Of course, Duane outweighs me by at least a hundred pounds. Dragging Max along wouldn't have been quite the same challenge. And it must have been before sunset when he did it, giving him more light to see by.

But I'm not going to think about this. It makes no difference. I need to get him out before the bluff swallows us both.

"Max," I tell him, "I'm going to count to three. On three, take a deep breath, follow me, and swim forward as hard as you can. Ready?"

He doesn't answer. But his fingers tighten around mine.

"Okay. One. Two. *Three.*"

I inhale. I thrust my head and shoulders into the water. I slither forward, groping against the cold rock. When I'm completely submerged, and when I can't feel anything in front of me but cold and wet, I kick hard against the rock.

We're moving. Max's weight tugs against me, a giant anchor. But I feel him trying to move too, awkward little jerks when the backward pull goes slack.

We must be through the cave mouth by now. I tilt upward.

My head bashes stone. The shock of the pain almost makes me suck in water.

No. We're still inside.

I have to angle downward again, even though my whole body is begging to claw its way up, up, up. Just a little farther. I hope.

Two more strong kicks.

My lungs are starting to ache.

Again, I angle upward.

This time there's nothing above me. Are we out of the cave? My senses are erased; there's nothing left to tell me. Just water in my ears, the taste of the river in my mouth.

I kick hard. We must be almost to the surface now. Almost.

My body screams for air.

I can't do this. I can't. I'm running out of time.

I open my eyes. The muddy water burns. I can't see a thing. If there was something, even a tiny flicker of light, hope of reaching it might pull me those last few feet. But there's nothing.

One more kick. I reach up with my right hand.

Wind whips my skin as it breaks the surface.

There.

Please, my whole body screeches. *Please.*

With both hands, both arms, I burst upward, shoving myself out of the water. Gasping.

It's all here. It's all still here. Air. Land. The whole living world.

I blink up at the sky. There are so many stars.

And I'm not holding Max's hand.

The fact hits me like an avalanche.

My body took over. It needed both arms, it needed every inch of itself to survive. And so I let go.

I thrash around, scanning the muddy water.

In the distance, knee-deep in the Bend, I make out Chuck and Maeve and Duane. I turn my back to them and scan the black waves. The water might as well be tar.

It's the last thing I want to do, but I take a deep breath and plunge back under, reaching out with both hands.

My fingers strike something.

I grab on.

Yank upward.

Max breaks the surface beside me.

He's gagging. Coughing. Making enough noise that I'm terrified one of the Oldies will hear. But we're both breathing this wet summer air.

"Come on," I tell him, keeping close to the wall of the bluff, pulling him toward the edge of the water.

I crawl up onto the muddy ground as far from the Oldies as we can get. When I glance in their direction, I see that they've got Maeve surrounded. She's holding something else, something sharp and shiny, in her fist. Jan Lundberg's pocketknife, I suppose. She's still buying us time.

Max drags himself onto the ground after me. We're waterlogged, shuddering, clothes hanging on us like weights. The silver key around my neck is gone, probably sinking to the mud of the riverbed right now.

"All right?" I whisper.

Max doesn't answer. He coughs, retching onto the sodden grass.

One of the Oldies shouts something. Faces swivel in our direction.

They see us. Both of us.

I yank Max to his feet.

"Run." I shove him ahead of me. "Go. Just get into the woods and hide. *Run.*"

Max looks too breathless to argue. He staggers ahead of me into the trees.

I glance back.

Maeve is speaking loudly, but I can't catch the words. My heart's thumping too hard. River water dribbles from my ears. I see her make a movement just before Chuck lunges toward her.

But my grandpa's eyes are fixed on me.

I'm a deer in a scope.

For a second, my heart stops, like a hunter's bullet has already torn through.

But then it thuds again, and I dive into the woods.

20

Sticks and bracken crack under me. Leaves lash my face. The night's getting darker, and I can't tell where Max went or where to safely set my feet. I duck just in time to keep from smashing my skull into a branch that looms out of the shadows, and my knees buckle, sending me forward onto my freezing hands.

My body's sputtering out. Too much effort. Too much panic. And the aftereffects of the drugs in that coffee still cling to me like my own cold, wet clothes.

I shove myself upright and run harder. My shoes skid in the slippery mud and heaps of dead leaves, scrambling, racing, until one foot hits a hollow space between two jutting roots, and my ankle snaps sideways.

The shot of pain is so sudden, I hit the ground before I'm sure what happened. I wrench my body around, patting at my ankle. Is it broken? Sprained? I try to set both feet on the ground and push upright, but another bolt of pain collapses me fast as a flipped switch.

For a few heartbeats, I huddle there, wet and gasping.

And then I hear footsteps. Already so close.

I know these footsteps. I've heard them stepping in through the kitchen door of our old brick house. I've heard them thump up the stairs to my bedroom to ask if I feel like some pie down at Lou's, or if I want to go for an early morning stroll.

I hold my breath and flatten myself to the ground.

Maybe he won't hear me.

Maybe he won't see.

But Grandpa's always had sharp eyes.

Another step brushes closer.

I freeze.

He gives that tutting little sigh—the noise he used to make when he'd find me sitting up way past my bedtime, huddled in bed with my reading lamp and a book—and I know it's too late.

"Lucia," he says softly.

I shove myself to my feet. Pain spears up my leg, but I force myself to stand straight, to keep my face still. To look like I could outrun him at any moment.

I turn and face my grandpa.

In the moonlight that drips through the trees, he looks gray and insubstantial, like something shaped out of fog. Like a ghost.

"You're okay?" he asks.

I almost laugh. I am light-years from okay.

I glance to either side. No sign of Chuck or Duane; at least not yet. But I don't know what they have planned, or what might be creeping up behind me through the trees. Because I don't know them.

I thought I did. I'd have bet my entire life on it.

Maybe I have.

I take a step backward, fighting to keep the wince off my face.

"It was you," I say, as clearly as I can. "All of you. You killed that kid." I swallow hard, so my voice won't break. "Neil."

It's a statement, not a question. But I still want Grandpa to argue. Amend my words. Give some explanation that would erase everything I've finally uncovered and wash it all away.

But he doesn't speak. He just looks at me, and I hear him take a deep breath.

"Did you do it the same way? Like you were going to do to Max right now?" I ask. "Did you drug him and leave him in the cave?"

Grandpa keeps still for another moment, and I wonder if he's still not going to answer. But then he says, firmly and slowly, "He didn't feel a thing."

My knees almost give out under me. I ball my fists, and I breathe, and I wait.

Grandpa goes on, speaking carefully, setting out each awful word like it's something that could shatter. "Marina always knew what to use. He went to sleep. Totally painless."

"And before Neil, and after Neil . . ." I prompt. "The same thing. All those people. It wasn't Jake, or Kyle, or any of those other stupid kids with their bonfires. It was *you*. Over and over again."

Grandpa raises one hand, like you do when you're cornering a wild animal. "We never wanted to do this, you know," he says, in that reasonable voice. "My father, my grandfather, all the way back. No one wanted to." He pauses. "It was never about wanting to hurt anyone. It was just about trying to save this place."

I hear myself make a sound that's not a laugh, but that's not anything else either. "Did you think I'd never figure it out?" I demand. "Even when you tried it with my own friend?"

"Of course not," says Grandpa. "Smart cookie like you? Nah." He gives that dry grin. The one that always used to make me smile back. Now it makes my heart stutter. "We just hoped you'd see how much there is to lose," he says. "The museum. Our heritage. Our family. All our families. The entire town." He takes a step closer. "That's why I knew you would understand."

"Understand?" I want to scream. I want to scream and scream and scream. "You *knew* I'd understand? You were going to kill him!"

"We were going to let him die. There's a difference."

Grandpa takes another small step closer. I step backward,

landing wrong, sucking a breath through my teeth as the pain sears upward.

I've given myself away.

"I need you to listen now, Lucia," says Grandpa, with another step. "He knew too much. And he would never understand. He's not part of this place. But you . . ."

Before I see what's coming, before I can try to scramble away on my throbbing ankle, Grandpa's hand lashes out. He grasps me by the wrist. I start to turn, but his other hand locks around my opposite arm.

I know too much.

Grandpa's hands are big. Astonishingly strong. He's holding on to me so hard, it feels like he's pulling me straight down into the ground.

"We did this for you," he says.

I try to wrench backward, but I can't even budge. My arms are locked in his grip. My ankle pulses.

"For *me*?" I push the words through my teeth.

"For you. For this place." Grandpa's voice seems to grow rougher with each word. "We were just trying to hold on."

The night wind whips past. I'm still drenched with river water, and my whole body begins to shudder. With cold. With dread. With rage. "Did you think I was going to take this over for you?" I spit. "Carry on this *tradition*?"

Grandpa's face, so close to mine, is getting paler. There's tightness around his mouth. Around his eyes.

"We thought . . . if you stayed . . ." he says, gripping my arms even harder, "if you settled down with another Black Point kid, someone who belonged here . . . Maybe." His voice grows rougher with each word. "But honestly, I always kind of hoped . . . I always hoped this part would die out with us."

He lets go of my arms.

And that's when I realize that Grandpa wasn't holding me still. He was holding himself upright.

He makes another sound, like the start of a word, choked off. His knees crash to the bracken. From there he sags to his side.

I watch his face in the dimness. His eyes are half closed. His chest jerks as it rises and falls. One arm wraps across his body, clutching the opposite shoulder.

His heart.

I know the signs. I've watched for them for years.

All the things inside me, all the moments and memories and habits and beliefs, wrench at me like invisible ropes. But those ropes are fraying now. I feel them snap and fall as I take a backward step.

I slide one shaking hand into my pocket and pull out my phone. Maybe I'll be lucky and catch a wisp of a signal.

But the screen doesn't even flicker on. Because I dove straight into the muddy floodwater with the phone in my pocket. Damn it.

I shove the dead thing back into my wet jeans.

Grandpa is lying in the moldering leaves, breathing hard.

He tilts his face in my direction. His eyes catch on me, wavering a few yards away.

I see a specter of the smile he always gets when he sets eyes on me. It slides on and off his face like a flickering light.

"Lucia," he says softly. "It's all right."

It's not all right.

Nothing is all right.

"I'm going to get you help," I tell him, because I can't just stand here and watch. And I can't get any closer, either. I take two more limping, backward steps on my flaming ankle. "I just have to find the road."

"No." Grandpa says. "This is better."

I take another step. "Which way is the road from here?"

Grandpa speaks again, but he's not answering me. "It should be me this time," he says. "Just have them give me to the water."

"I'm going," I tell him, and my voice is loud and firm.

"Lucia," he says. "Let it be."

But I've already turned away.

My ankle throbs as I stumble-hop in what I hope is the right direction. I crash through thorns, slide down muddy patches. I don't cry. I don't think. I just move.

No sounds around me but my own jagged footfalls. No trails, no familiar paths. Nothing but the stars, reaching weakly toward me from above the rustling trees. I can't tell which one is brightest. I don't know which way is north, or east, or up or down. I don't know my way home.

There is no way home anymore.

Finally, on the muddy side of a hill, I set my right foot down too hard, and the bolt of pain that goes through me knocks me to my knees.

I hunch there for a while, my face in the rotting leaves, my wet skin turning to ice. I try to keep my breaths from turning to sobs, but it's not working. I've lost everything. Including myself.

Around me, insects chirr. Breeze shuffles the leaves. And then, faint as the starlight, I catch the scent of smoke.

My throat tightens with fear. It's not the smell of a bonfire, wet wood and dead flesh.

It's the smell of a cigarette.

I stiffen.

Les?

I sit up, trying to stare in every direction at once. There's no sound, no other footsteps, no more old men chasing me through the trees. Just the smell of the cigarette—and, I swear, a whisper of some old-fashioned perfume.

I go silent. Barely breathing.

Several steps ahead of me, at the crest of the hillside, I see it. Something white. Something long and soft and lacy, trailing over the wet earth.

It wants me to follow.

But I can't.

I can't even stand up, let alone run. There's nothing left inside of me that I can burn to fuel my way.

The hem of the white skirt sweeps out of sight.

It's over.

There's nothing left for me. The future that I had planned, the life that flowed ahead of me like the river—it's gone. I could curl up here in the wet ferns and moss and never wake up.

I sag back into the dead leaves.

I'm stopped before I touch the ground.

Someone is holding my arm.

I whip to the side, expecting Grandpa, or one of the Oldies, the next awful turn in this nightmare.

There's no one there.

And still, I can feel it. I can feel a hand—a little smaller and much colder than Grandpa's—wrapping around my flesh, just above the elbow. Its grip is gentle but steady.

It pulls me to my feet.

With that hand holding me up, I manage one more limping step. Then another.

And another.

I—we—reach the crest of the hill. My ankle is still thudding like a drum, sending ripples of pain up my shin, but I'm moving forward. The body beside me helps bear my weight.

We start down the slope, through the box elders and oaks. The hand on my arm steers me. There's a gust of wind, and starlight shivers on the leaves, and again I catch the scents of perfume and cigarettes. In the shadows ahead of us, the woman in white leads the way.

I glance over again. From the corner of my eye, I swear I can see him: Pale T-shirt. Blue jeans. A boy about my age, with short hair and deep eyes.

Then I stumble, because I'm not watching the lumpy ground ahead, and his grasp holds me up.

"Thanks, Neil," I whisper.

He doesn't answer.

I turn toward him once more, but at the same second, the grip on my arm disappears, and suddenly I'm skidding down an incline into a stark, clear space.

A road. A dirt road.

I glance both ways.

Neil is gone.

Before I can be certain of anything else, there's a roar. An engine careening closer.

Blinding light crashes over me. Headlights. Too fast, too near for me to dive out of the way. I throw up my arms, as though they'll shield me, but I don't close my eyes. If something is coming for me now, I want to see it head-on.

There's a grind of brakes. The lights shudder and still.

The car stops a few feet away.

"Lucia!" shouts a voice through an open window. Maeve's voice. "Get in back!"

I stumble through the wall of white light to the side of her car.

My knees are liquid. My vision is seared.

I just manage to yank open the rear door.

And there's Max.

Max.

He's sprawled out across the wide seat, shoulders propped against the far door, half upright.

But he's alive.

His eyes hit me. A small, sleepy, unsteady smile begins to uncurl on his face.

"Valkyrie," he whispers.

I pull myself inside, slamming the door behind me. Then I grab his hand. It's cold. Muddy. So is mine.

We both hold on.

"My grandpa had a heart attack," I tell Maeve. "Up that hill, not too far from where you found me. He needs an ambulance."

Maeve gives a little nod. She doesn't speak.

The car speeds along the dirt road, veering through the trees.

I turn back toward Max. His head lolls against the seat. But his eyes are open.

"I'm so sorry," I tell him softly. "I'm so sorry."

He tips his head toward me. His eyes are still bleary, low lidded, but they stay fixed firmly on my face. "Why're you sorry? You just saved me." With his free hand, he reaches into a pocket and tugs something out. Even in the dark of the back seat, I recognize the little drawstring pouch on a cord swinging from his fingers. Maeve's protective charm.

"As long as we stay together . . ." Max says. His words are

slurred. I hear his breathing deepen as he sinks into sleep.

I hope it's just sleep. I hope we've been quick enough. That there's still time.

The car swings around a curve, off the dirt road, onto the highway.

I glance out the windows.

We're not turning toward Black Point. We're heading north, toward another town, somewhere else. I don't know where Maeve will stop. But it will be a place that doesn't already know us. Where we can tell the police the truth without them covering it back up. Where we can get help, even if it's from strangers. Or because it's from strangers.

Max's grip has loosened a little, but his fingers are still woven through mine. I move my arm, bracing it against my leg, so that we can both rest without letting go.

Then I lean back against the seat too, watching the black-purple sky slide past the windows. Letting darkness and distance guide me away, toward something new.

September 12

Max,

I hope you won't mind that I'm writing to you. I'm doing it with an actual on-paper letter instead of trying to find you online or anything. This way, I'll never even know if you got the message. And if you don't want to hear from me, all you have to do is tear this up and I'll be gone again. No more reminders that I even exist.

Plus, it kind of feels right. It makes me feel like Neil must have felt, writing all those letters, hoping somebody would believe him.

And you did.

Anyway.

We never really got to talk, after everything. I understand why. But I still would have at least liked to tell you I was sorry. I mean, I told you I was sorry that night, in the back of Maeve's car, but I'm guessing you might not remember. I hope you don't remember a lot of things from that night.

Sometimes I wish I could forget it all too. But I need to remember it. All of it. Because that's how I know it's over.

Mom and I have left Black Point. She didn't know about all of this, about what was going on all along. Or at least that's what she says. Maybe it's true. I mean, I didn't know, and I was right there. I didn't see it. Not until you showed me.

The museum is permanently closed. Grandpa's whole estate was seized, which includes our house, the collection, a bunch of businesses. Maybe it will all be sold. I heard your aunt left too, so the hotel is empty again. Maybe the whole town will empty out. Die off. It's probably time.

I'm sure you already know this part, but Chuck and Duane and Les are in prison. Maeve got some kind of deal for being the one to turn everybody in, but that's all I know about her. And Grandpa's gone.

When the EMTs finally got out to that spot in the woods that night, they were already way too late. The Oldies admitted it. They'd followed Grandpa's wishes. Gave the water his ashes and bones. My mom had his name added to Grandma Kay's headstone in the Black Point Cemetery, even though he's not there. But it makes things seem final, I guess.

I'll never see that headstone. It doesn't matter either.

We live in Iowa now. Des Moines. Not a big city, really, but big enough that we can sort of disappear. I'm finishing high school online, so mostly,

I just stay inside our new little house, but if I ever do go out, I can walk down any street without a single person knowing my name, or why I'm here, or who I am.

It's good.

It seems funny to me now. That all I wanted was to make things just like they used to be. And now all I want is something brand-new. I don't know. Maybe if you take away all the things and places and people that defined you, it's easier to figure out who you are.

Next year I'll start college. I want to head someplace bigger than Des Moines. My first choice is Minneapolis. Someplace where everything can feel fresh. Someplace where I don't know anybody at all.

Except you.

That's the other reason I'm writing. It's a big city, and maybe you'll be going somewhere else for school or whatever anyway. But I still wanted you to know. Because if we happen to run into each other, and if you want to act like we've never even met, I would totally get it.

The last thing I wanted to say, and I know that it's weird, is—thank you.

Really. You're the one who stopped everything

from ever happening again. Hopefully Neil's family and Carole's family and everybody else feel like they have answers now. Even if they're not good ones. Maybe the ghosts have finally checked out of the hotel.

You helped them. You and Neil. You told the truth.

And you helped me see it too.

So. Thank you.

If you want to get in touch, my address is on the envelope.

And if you don't, I'll understand.

Lucia

September 19

Now I get to show you around MY town.

Can't wait.

—Max

ACKNOWLEDGMENTS

LOVE AND THANKS TO:

- Danielle Chiotti, who never lost faith in this book, or in me. I am so unbelievably lucky to have you in my corner. Huge additional thanks to Michael Stearns and everyone else at Upstart Crow Literary.
- My brilliant editor, Kristie Choi. Thank you for seeing straight to the core of this story and for making each step of the process feel like a dream. It was my lucky day when this book ended up in your hands. And to the whole team at Atheneum/Simon & Schuster—designer Karyn Lee, production editor Kaitlyn San Miguel, copyeditor Michelle Lippold, production manager Tatyana Rosalia, and everyone else making magic behind the scenes—thank you, thank you, thank you.
- Artist Jenna Barton, who created the cover of my wildest and creepiest dreams.

- Anne Greenwood Brown, Lauren Peck, Connie Kingrey Anderson, Jennifer Kaul, and Kristen Nelson, for seeing this one from beginning to end. It wouldn't be the book it is (and I wouldn't be the writer I am) without you.
- My fellow weirdos in Spooky Middle Grade (Hi, Spookies!), who make the publishing world a friendlier place.
- The Red Wing Public Library and its amazing staff. (And to Youth Services librarian Megan Seeland: Sorry you have to read another scary one.)
- The entire Minnesota book community: Authors and illustrators, bookstores and booksellers, librarians and educators, organizers and activists and readers. There's nowhere I'd rather be.
- Wardruna, for the perfect writing soundtrack.
- My family. To all the Cobians, Swansons, McHargs, Nelsons, Betzels, and Wests: So grateful to have you as the roots and branches of my tree. Mom and Dad, thanks for still being proud of every little thing I do—and thank you for all the help with childcare. And finally, especially, to Ryan, Beren, and Vivien. You three are my home.